King's Mansion

by Barbara Drumright

DORRANCE
PUBLISHING CO
EST. 1920
PITTSBURGH, PENNSYLVANIA 15238

Dorrance Publishing Co
585 Alpha Drive
Pittsburgh, PA 15238
Visit our website at *www.dorrancebookstore.com*

ISBN: 978-1-6491-3492-9
eISBN: 978-1-6491-3909-2

Who would have thought that I, Amber Gold, would end up standing here and looking down on the small cottage where I lived the first sixteen years of my life. I think about how lucky I am to be living in the mansion that I dreamed about when I was a child.

My mother and father were never rich; however, they made me feel like I was the best loved and cared for person in the world. I grew up with a lot of love and security that even now makes me smile. Mother always made sure that my clothes were cleaned and ironed. I always had a ribbon in my long hair. I can remember my Mother brushing my hair at night and telling me how lucky I was to have hair the color of gold. My name is Amber Elizabeth Gold, and everyone called me Amber. My hair is golden blonde, and my eyes are green. My Father always said that when I got mad, they turned a dark green, like the richest grass in the Springtime of the year.

Since my first memories we had lived at the cottage house on the King Estate. My father was the caretaker and did the groundwork and maintained a large garden for the entire household. My mother helped in the big house and took care of the flowers for all the arrangements needed for all the parties that the King family was continually having for friends and family.

I first saw the son, Slate King, from a distance. He was never home as a child. He was always at various boarding schools or abroad with his parents. I heard from the servants that the young master was due home for two weeks. How can I describe that first look at Slate King? He was very tall, unruly black ebony hair, tanned to a golden brown, with eyes so blue you could swim in the depts and never want to get out.

He was twenty now and training to take over the family empire. It was said that he had already amassed a large fortune of his own and was quite the ladies' man, and the most eligible catch around. All Mothers were trying to attract Slate to their daughters, all to no avail. Mr. King did not want to be caught.

I daydreamed a lot about Slate King. Of course, I was only 16 and still a child in thoughts as well as body. Mother said I was a late bloomer. I despaired every time I looked in the mirror. My breasts were too small, my eyes too big for my face. Nothing seemed to fit. At least my hair matched my name. It was long and blonde. When I helped Mother at the mansion, I had to keep my hair tucked up in a bun, which continually kept falling down.

I caught glimpses of Master Slate from time to time. He was always with friends and took no notice of me, who I am sure he would have considered a mere child.

A coming-home party was being given for Slate, and the servants had been working for weeks to get ready for the big event. I was to serve and help clean up after the party. Over 300 guests were invited. The day of the party finally arrived. It was truly a beautiful day. I slipped away in the early afternoon. My favorite place was through the woods, across the little bridge and then follow the sound of water until you see the little waterfall. I pulled off my shoes, and dangled my feet in the water. It was so peaceful. I was dreaming about Master Slate. In my dreams he looked at me and it was love and lust all rolled into one look. I heard a noise and opened my eyes; I thought that I had to still be dreaming, looking up into the sun I saw Slate with the sun brilliant behind his head. He was smiling and looking so handsome. I could not say anything, just looked at him and wished for the 100th time that I was beautiful and had beautiful clothes to wear so he would notice me.

As he smiled and said hello, time seemed suspended as our eyes met and held. As Slate started to speak, I picked up my shoes and bolted. I fled like a startled deer into the woods. His call to wait that he would not hurt me only made me run faster.

Slate wondered who the girl was, her clothes as he remembered were plain and out of style. Possibly one of the girls from the village who had slipped on King property for a swim and forgotten the time. She was so small, possibly only reaching his shoulders and probably very young. He cautioned himself to remember that the girl was in all likelihood untouched and he made a practice not to waste his time on virgins. He could still remember his first virgin at the age of sixteen, the girl was fifteen and for a time he thought he would be forced to marry the girl, but luckily her period started and he was off the hook. His Father sent him away for a period of time and took care of the situation with some well-placed funds in the bank for the family. Since that time, he had steered clear of shy untouched girls in the village.

Slate had always had the best of everything. His parents had lost two children before they finally succeeded with Slate. From the very first, everything revolved around Slate. He was sent to the finest boarding schools where he excelled in all sports, as well as grades. At the age of 13 he went abroad for the first time. This was the time he discovered girls. Life became even better. Slate loved them well and left them wanting more.

At the age of 20 he was getting restless and tired of his lifestyle. Now he left the crowded party room and made his way out to the balcony. He lit a cigarette and reflected on his day. After his morning ride he had made his way to his favorite spot since he was a child. The waterfall seemed smaller than he remembered. Laying by the pool of water was a small, beautiful child, sleeping so innocently with a half-smile on her face turned toward the evening sun. Her hair was like a halo fanning out around her small face and the color was pure gold. He stood for a period of time quietly observing the girl. Slate was very curious about the color of her eyes, with that gold hair he figured green. As he started walking closer, he stepped on a twig. The girl came slowly awake. He would have won his bet; her eyes were bright green with long lashes fanning out into a question mark. Her startled glance settled on Slate as in a dream. He wished that she had not run away so quickly.

Since his return home René Blake, whose parents owned the adjoining property, had not left him alone René was tall with jet black hair, full red lips that pouted a lot, and very large breasts that she showed to the best advantage in all her clothes. Her dress today of red silk stopped only at the point of being indecent. He had danced three dances with her already tonight. She made no secret of the fact that she would not resist any advances made by Slate. Slate had not pressed the point; he was not sure he wanted to start something with René, even though, he was sure her favors had been sampled by many in the village.

Well, he had been gone long enough and was sure his mother was getting anxious for him to return to his coming home party. Still, he could not get the girl with the golden hair out of his mind. She was surely not his type, but he still wondered who she was and made a mental note to ask his mother if she knew who the girl was after his description was given.

As Slate stepped back into the party room, René instantly came forward. She had been looking for him for the better part of ten minutes. She had turned down at least three dance partners in that period of time but had decided that she had to have Slate and his money. He was by far the most exciting and attractive man she had ever encountered and René had been experimenting with the male animal for years.

René instantly latched onto Slate, at the same time Slate saw the girl from the waterfall carrying a tray of empty glasses to the kitchen. He wanted to go to the girl at that time; however, René would not let him go without a dance. He realized he was trapped for the present. After two dances he went in search for the mystery girl, however he did not find her. She had vanished.

The next morning, he questioned his parents about the girl. His mother had no idea who he was talking about as they hired lots of people from the village to serve and help out for the numerous parties they were famous for, so he was unable to get any information.

You take for granted all the wonderful times in your life and never think they can end in a mere second of time. My father was cutting down a large tree that had been partially uprooted by a recent storm. He had used the axle and cut around the tree but misjudged where the tree would fall and could not get out of the way. We found him when he did not show up for the evening meal. One of the sharp limbs that had been exposed by the storm had buried in my Father's neck and he had bled to death. It was really a very hard time for Mother and me; but, knew he would want us to carry on. After the funeral, we were told that we could stay at our little home for another month and $500.00 would be given to us. We were sure we could find something suitable by that time and the money seemed like a God sent to us. After looking for weeks we finally found a small house close to the village for $55.00 per month. At the time, Mother and I thought this was a large sum of money and we would want for nothing if we managed wisely. We borrowed a wagon and moved our small belongings to the house and set up housekeeping.

My mother was never a strong person and it seemed after Father died, she did not have the will to go on. She tried for my sake to keep going and to do what had to be done. My Father had always protected Mother so she would not worry.

We quickly found out that the $500.00 was not going to last that long. I was now 17 and filling out at an alarming rate. It seemed that all my dresses were getting tighter at the top and Mother kept taking them out and adding extra material. The money was going fast. Rent payment, buying material, buying food, along with the prescriptions and the doctor visits for Mother. We had found out that Mother had a heart problem and had to take it easy.

The only way to make ends meet was for me to get a job. Mother was firmly opposed to this ideal. She had insisted that I keep up my schooling and was teaching me at home, so I would be able to graduate with my class the next year. I slipped out early the next morning, determine to get some kind of a job, as our money would be gone within two months. I first checked with the market where I purchased our food — no openings, no job available. These were the words I heard at each place I inquired about work. After hours of walking the streets I saw a help wanted sign at the Bar and Suds. I knew this was not the kind of place Mother would want me to work; but I had no choice and if I was offered the job, I would take it. I went inside and talked with the owner, Mr. Greenly. The job included cooking, doing the dishes, and cleaning up after the dinner trade had ended for the day. The job paid $5.00 per day; however, Mr. Greenly offered me a job as a server in the bar area where he said I would make considerably more money. I peeped in the bar area and saw the pretty bar maids carrying beer and whiskey to the gentlemen that were at the bar and tables. I saw how the men touched and slapped the backsides of the barmaids as they went by, and I knew I would not be able to tolerate working in the bar. I started work the next day in the kitchen.

The work was hard, but I was able to be home with Mother and get her evening meal and give her the medicine she needed before going to work. We would go over the lessons that Mother assigned me each day. Mother thought my job was at the food market where I cleaned and stocked the goods each evening. I made sure I stayed in the kitchen at work and never went out into the bar area except sometimes during lunch when there was a different crowd. At night, I could hear the laughter and shrieks from the serving girls that worked in the bar.

One evening, Mr. Greenly came into the kitchen and told me I would have to help out in the bar that evening. He had two girls out and had to have at least one more person working. I flatly refused to even consider the offer. However, Mr. Greenby made it plain that in order to keep my job I would have to help out or I could leave and not come back. I could not afford to lose my job since we depended on every penny that I made to get by. I put on the uniform that he furnished and tried to pull the blouse up and make it decent. As I ventured into the bar area, I noticed Jim Stanley at a table. Jim had gone to the same school that I attended for a short period of time, but he had been expelled for continually getting into trouble. He had been older than most of his classmates at school and since he was so big, he was always doing cruel things to the smaller children. He had tried on more than one occasion to get me to go out with him. He finally decided that I thought I was too good for him. Now, he looked up and saw me and a big grin showed on his beefy face. I took orders and served beer to some of the tables nearest to the door. I tried to avoid going to the table where Jim was seated.

Slate was sitting in the back of the bar. He had come here to escape his mother and Rená. The campaign had become very serious to get Slate. It seemed every time he turned around Rená was at his house or he was having to escort his mother to Rená's for a visit. He was sure his mother was unaware of Rená's true nature and would probably have been shocked to know that Rená had been with quite a few of the young common men from the village, if all the talk was true that Slate had heard from various friends. Slate concluded from the actions of Rená when they were alone that all the talk was indeed true. She had practically raped him on more than one occasion. It wasn't that Slate did not like women, the simple fact was — Slate enjoyed being the aggressor. He was tired of women falling at his feet because he was rich or because of his good looks. He noticed that the bar was busy for a weeknight and with only two barmaids, they were on the run to fill the orders.

The barmaid was keeping Slate's glass filled and giving him a generous view of her large breasts when she leaned down with the tray. She had also indicated that she got off at 1:00 a.m. if Slate would like to hang around. Slate heard some commotion from the other side of the tavern and saw the other barmaid with a tray in her hand waiting tables. She was unsuccessfully trying to dodge the hands that reached out to pat her backside as she delivered the beers to the tables. Her hair was hidden under the scarf pulled very tightly around her face; however, the loose clothes did not completely hide her young and petite figure. She seemed really out of her depth, and Slate wondered why she would be working at a place like this. As she passed close to his table he could have sworn she was on the verge of tears, however no one was forcing her to do the work she was doing, so he figured he must have been wrong about the tears.

Amber was wondering how she was going to make it through the night. She had worked the tables some during the dinner crowd but had never worked at night when the clientele changed so drastically. She was certain the men thought she was a loose woman, but she had to think of her mother and the medicine she must buy weekly with her checks and the rent also had to paid. She could not afford to lose this job, so with tears practically making their way to the surface she continued trying to serve the beer and keep the men from touching her. She could not understand why they were fooling with her. She had made herself as unattractive as possible before coming from the kitchen. As Amber passed by Slate sitting there looking at her with a half-smile on his face, her heart melted every time she looked into his eyes. It seemed to Slate that she was startled to see him as she hurried by his table.

I had heard a lot of stories about Jim from the other girls at school and I was afraid to go out with him. Since school I had lost track of him but had heard he got a girl with child and had been forced to marry her. Jim had always had the hots for Amber ever since high school, but she was stuck up and would not give him the time of day. Seeing her in a place like this meant she had shore fallen down off her high horse. Maybe he would buy her for the night. He would love to put it to her and hear her cries of delight as he straddled her small body and split her open. He would do it to her, over and over. Just thinking about finally having Miss High and Mighty was giving him a "hard on." It seemed that this did not happen much these days, as his wife of three years was fat from two kids and no exercise. It seemed that all he heard from home was crying and whining from the wife and kids.

Jim now saw something he had wanted for years and nothing was going to stand in his way tonight. He was thinking he just might keep her on the side and use her whenever he wanted. Amber hated to go by his table but had to deliver the beer to the customers. As she went by Jim's table, he reached out and grabbed her. The beer spilled and slipped from her hand. The next thing she knew she was sitting on Jim's lap. She tried in vain to get away, but Jim only laughed and tightened his hold on her waist. He reached up and ripped off the scarf that held Amber's hair. Instantly her long blonde hair spilled down around her shoulders. Slate, still sitting at his table, had watched the man grab Amber and her attempts to get away. Slate slowly got to his feet and started over to the table. Jim was telling Amber by this time what he planned for her and him that night and other nights to come if she pleased him.

By this time, Amber was in tears. No one seemed to care that she was trying to get away. No one came to her aid. Jim said he could not wait any longer and started pulling her across the room and up the stairs. Slate reached Amber as Jim pulled her up the steps. Slate told Jim that a mistake had been made that he had already purchased her services for the night. Amber could only stare at Slate as he said these words. Slate reached out and got Amber and put her behind him. Jim was not going to be put off, he could already see all his plans for Amber going out the window. Jim swung and connected with Slate's jaw; however, Slate did not go down as expected. Slate landed one hard blow to Jim's nose and Jim slowly went down with blood streaming from his nose. Amber knew she had to get out of the tavern while she still could. She ran out the door with Slate close behind her. Her hair was flying out behind her as she ran. Slate caught her as she rounded the corner, she jerked away and continued running. As she started across the street her foot slipped and the next thing she knew, she was flying through the air and landed hard on her back. The wind was knocked from her and she laid there trying to get her breath and to come back, however she was still in a twilight state. Slate had saw Amber fall and reached her side at about the time she landed. He was fearful that something was broken, but upon careful examination she seemed to be ok and was coming around. Amber came to and saw Slate bending over her and running his hands over her body. His touch was so gentle, it felt so right somehow. Slate saw her eyes open and ask if she was alright as he helped her up. Amber sagged against Slate's body. Slate could not believe how perfectly she fit into his arms. Amber then remembered what Slate had told Jim about purchasing her services for the evening. Amber stiffened and tried to draw her body away from him. Slate wondered why she went from hot to cold so fast! He knew he could offer her a lot more than the other man at the tavern and he would definitely treat her better.

Amber did not know what she was going to do. She was sure she had lost her job and would be unable to pay for her mother's medicine. Slate heard her sign and when he looked down, he could have sworn he again saw tears on her long lashes. Slate volunteered to walk her home or take her anywhere she would like to go. Amber declined both offers and said goodbye. Slate followed her down the street at a loss for words. No girl or woman had ever turned down Slate King. As Amber turned the corner and into the gate leading to the little house they rented, Slate followed. When Amber reached the door, she turned on Slate and ask him to leave. She was very upset and could only think of trying and finding some work the next day. As Slate stood there, the door was slammed in his face.

Slate knew he would make her regret her actions this night, however walking home all he could think about was folding Amber into his arms and protecting her. He could not understand where these feelings came from, as Amber could take care of herself. The next morning

Amber said nothing to her mother about losing her job and set out directly after breakfast to find some kind of work so she would have some money coming in each week. Amber tried the marketplace, post office, dress shop, and some small shops on main street. No one had any openings. Amber thought about going to the tavern and begging for her job back. She knew she would have to work in the bar if she returned and knew she would not be able to handle working there anymore. Late in the day she made the climb up the hill to King's mansion, hoping they might have something in the kitchen. The housekeeper had nothing; however, she had heard that the Blake household had an opening for a maid. Amber slowly left the King's mansion and headed with dragging feet to the Blake estate.

The housekeeper did indeed have an opening for a maid as Miss Rená had ran off another maid only the previous day. Amber was told she had the job and the hours would be from 7:00 a.m. until 6:30 p.m. Monday through Saturday with Sunday off. Her duties would include cleaning all the upstairs each day and at the beck and call of Miss Rená. Amber was given a uniform and told to show up the next morning and was told to be on time. Amber told her mother her job had changed to days, no more night work. Amber kept silent about her new employment and put on a happy face for her mother.

That day while Amber had been looking for a job, Slate had a business deal that could not wait. Slate would be out of town for five to seven days. Mr. King had passed away the previous summer and all the estate business now fell for Slate to handle.

Amber settled into her new job. The work was very hard, but she knew better than to complain, as she needed this job desperately. Rená was a very demanding employer. She wanted all her gowns aired each day and mended and pressed as needed. All her shoes had to be brushed and new scented tissues stuffed in each shoe every day. Her bathwater had to be heated each day and carried up the stairs in buckets. After the bath, the same procedure had to be done. All the water had to be carried downstairs and emptied out the back door. By the end of the day, Amber walked home with the world on her shoulders. If she thought of Slate, it was only occasionally with the knowledge that he was out of her reach. She could dream, but the real world waited for her each day.

Amber's day had gone very badly, it seemed that no one in the house could please Miss Rená. She had been in a foul mood for days. The servants said she was mad that Mr. Slate had gone out of town and had not dropped her a note or told her when he left town. The talk was that Mr. Slate was due back that night and Rená had already made a trip over to see Mrs. King and invited her and Slate over for brunch the next day.

Amber had to stay late and do some repair work on a new gown that Miss Rená had purchased the previous day. The next morning when Amber arrived at work, everyone was very busy getting ready for the brunch with Mrs. King and Slate. Miss Rená could be heard screaming down the stairs for her bath water and her gown needed to be pressed again. Her hair had to be brushed and arranged over and over again. At the last minute she decided to change gowns again and Amber had to press yet another gown. When Mrs. King and Slate were announced, Rená hurried down the stairs. Rená had decided to wear her sea green gown with the wide lace trim around the neck, which was cut very low and emphasized her charms to the fullest. Her hair was put up with small curls escaping on each side. She knew the dress set off her dark hair to perfection. As she started down the stairs, she saw Slate and his mother at the bottom waiting. Slate had on a dark blue morning coat with lighter colored pants with a white shirt opened at the throat—Rená could not take her eyes off Slate—she must have him.

Slate was in a very bad frame of mind. His business dealings had gone well, and he had made a lot of money for the King empire. His Father would have been very proud of Slate. Since his Father had died, Slate had taken over all the family businesses and had pushed himself to make everything more profitable. He had been traveling for long periods of time and now wanted a change. He was not sure what direction this change was but wanted something more from life than constantly on the go and making more money than he could ever spend. It seemed that Slate could do no wrong in the business world, but his personal life was a different story. So, this was his frame of mind when his mother dragged him over to Rená's for brunch.

Rená turned her full charm on Slate and his mother. The food was served, and small conversation was made between the three people. Rená mentioned that she simply had to throw a welcome home party for Slate that would last for days. Rená also realized that her family money was getting lower and lower and that she was going to have to get Slate to propose soon. Her dressmaker had asked her for money last week before her new gowns had been delivered. It was only Rená quick thinking hinting that she would soon be Mrs. Slate King that kept the dressmaker at bay and the gowns delivered on credit. She knew that she had to make this happen quickly, or everything would go wrong for her.

Meanwhile, Amber was left upstairs trying to put things back in order and hanging up all the gowns that had been thrown on the floor. Amber knew that each gown would have to be pressed again before hanging them back up. The bath water still had to emptied, bucket by bucket. Trying to finish sooner Amber started with two full buckets down the stairs. She was being very careful, but one of the buckets slipped from her hand and the bucket of water went banging down the stairs. Amber watched the bucket and water falling on the steps and on the carpet below and knew she would not make it home till late to fix supper for her mother. Amber bit her lip hard to keep the tears from coming. Rená heard the noise and instantly ran out into the hall, when she saw the mess that Amber had made, she started screaming at the top of her lungs. Amber's pay would be docked to pay for the carpet and Amber was to clean up every trace of water on the carpet and wood. She was to then wax the wood floors by hand until you could see your face in the wood. Amber was afraid to say anything because of the fear of losing her job. Slate and his mother ventured out to the hall and Mrs. King was surprised at the manner and screams of Rená. This was no way to talk to your servants. Mrs. King had only observed Rená as a very gentle spoken lady on all occasions. This was a new side of Rená that Mrs. King had not observed.

Slate was beside himself with anger that Rená would act in this way. It was plain that the girl did not mean to drop the bucket. Slate also noticed that the buckets were too heavy for a small slip of a girl like Amber. Slate was also surprised that Amber was working for Rená. He figured she had gone back to the tavern the next day. Slate had thought he had driven the girl from his mind but upon seeing her again, knew it was a losing battle.

Amber wished the floor would open up and swallow her as she saw Slate and his mother coming into the hall. If only Slate was not so big and powerful looking. His dark hair had been combed earlier but a wave had worked its way free and was curling over his forehead. Amber noticed that he was very angry and assumed the fault lay in her for causing all the commotion. She moved back a step when Slate got close to her. Rená seeing that she was making a fool out of herself, told Amber to get back upstairs and finish her duties. Rená apologized to Mrs. King and Slate for losing her temper but said she had only wanted everything perfect for Slate's homecoming.

On the way home, Mrs. King was very quiet. She was beginning to think that she had misjudged Rená. She was thinking that maybe Rená was not the right choice for her only son.

Amber arrived home very late that night broken in spirit and very tired. Her mother had tried to fix supper and had retired to the tiny bedroom and was sleeping. In the small kitchen, careful not to wake her mother, Amber finally gave in to the grieve that she was feeling. She was only 17 years old but felt 100. She had no life, only work and more work. Amber did not often give in, but it seemed the whole weight of the world was on her small shoulders. Amber eventually raised herself from the kitchen table and give herself a small shake and thought she must not allow herself to feel sorry for herself or she would be lost forever. She still had her health and her loving Mother that helped all she could This was enough to keep her going.

Slate had also done some soul searching and had decided to find out more about the mystery girl. The next morning, before anyone was stirring in the household, Slate was up and dressed. Eager for the day to begin. His first stop was to the tavern where he had observed her working. He found that Amber had worked at the tavern for a year, cooking in the kitchen and had only served in the bar that one night before she fled, running from the tavern. His next stop was to the little house where he had followed Amber that night so long ago. Mrs. Gold answered his knock and let him in. Slate instantly saw the resemblance between Mrs. Gold and her daughter. Slate introduced himself to Mrs. Gold. She remembered Slate as a small boy and as a young gentleman when her husband had worked for the King's. Slate was surprised to learn that Mr. Gold had worked for the king family until his death. Mrs. Gold interrupted her speech with a spasm of coughs. Slate went to get her a drink of water, upon returning he noticed that the handkerchief had bright red blood on it from the coughing spell. Mrs. Gold confirmed his suspicious and told him about the heart problem that was getting worse every day. She told him that Amber knew she was sick but did not know the full details.

Slate listened to praise from Mrs. Gold about Amber. The girl had taken on the full responsibilities of all finances plus taking care of her since Mr. Gold had died. When Slate learned that Amber was only 17 and bearing all the heavy burden, he knew he must help.

Slate hurried home with his head full of plans. He knew that Mrs. Gold and Amber would not be comfortable in the big house, so he went to check on the condition of the cottage. His Father had built the cottage for his bride when they were first married. Later, as they prospered, he built the big house. Slate was very excited when he checked on the cottage and found everything in such wonderful condition. It would be perfect for Amber and her mother. His next stop was to the house to talk with his mother. He told his mother about Amber and her mother and the burden that Amber had been carrying for so long. He also told his mother that Amber was the girl at Rená's that had dropped the bucket down the stairs. His mother instantly put into motion a complete cleaning from top to bottom of the cottage and additional furniture to be moved from the big house to the cottage.

By the next afternoon the cottage was ready for Amber and her mother. Slate waited for the next morning to come. He waited until he was sure that Amber had left for work before going to see Mrs. Gold. He told her his plans to move them to the cottage. Slate stressed that they would be doing him a big favor, as the cottage needed someone to live there and look after things properly. Mrs. Gold was not taken in by Slate's story but felt this was a God sent because Amber could not go on as she was doing. Mrs. Gold accepted Slate's offer and he started getting things packed up to move them. Mrs. Gold had only a few cherished pieces of furniture that she wanted to move, so the packing process was very swift. Slate wanted to have Mrs. Gold installed comfortably at the cottage before Amber came home. Slate went back to the empty house that evening to wait for Amber to get home. It was after 6 p.m. and already dark before Amber came slowly down the lane to the house.

Amber's day had been very bad as Rená was taking her anger out on the girl and anyone else that got in her way. It had been all Amber could do to hold her tongue at the continuous insults and duties that Rená found for her to do and the rest of the staff. But Amber knew, she could not afford to lose this job, so she had again stayed late and finished chore after endless chore for Rená. She was on the complete verge of crying as she was so exhausted but knew she must put up a brave front for her mother. When Amber opened the door and saw Slate sitting by the fireplace, she thought she was dreaming. She had pictured him so many times in her mind. Her next thought was something had happened to her mother. Slate quickly assured her that all was well and that he would tell her what was happening if she would only sit down and listen. Slate knew he had to handle the next few minutes very carefully in order to get her to come to the cottage. He had to make sure Amber did not feel he was sorry for her or giving them charity. Slate explained that his mother had been looking for someone to stay at the cottage and keep it up and to help around the big house as needed. Slate told her he had talked with Mrs. Gold and since she knew Amber would want the position, she had already been installed at the cottage. Slate had remained at the house to take Amber when she got home as Mrs. Gold did not know how to reach her.

Amber was at a loss for words. She could not believe that this was happening. She told Slate she would accept his proposition only if she could work for their rent at the cottage. Slate readily agreed than escorted Amber to the cottage.

Meanwhile, Rená's plans to get Slate were not going good at all. Ever since the breakfast brunch, Mrs. King had not been as friendly and was not helping Rená at all in getting Slate. Mrs. Kings attitude had noticeably cooled toward her, since her unladylike behavior over the bucket incident. Rená was getting desperate for Slate and the money that would be hers on becoming his wife. The same night that Amber was moving, Rená laid awake for hours plotting her next move and eventually becoming Slate's wife and mistress of King's mansion. Rená had punished that silly girl over and over with every possible chore since the stupid girl had dropped the bucket, and this would continue in the morning.

Amber could not believe the change in her mother upon entering the cottage. A servant from the main house had already been down with supper for both women and Amber's was hot in the oven waiting for her. Slate dropped Amber off and declined to come in, knowing how tired she seemed to be. Amber and her mother talked late into the night. Amber slept until 9:30 a.m. the next morning. When she woke the sun seemed to be high in the sky. She had to think for a moment on where she was, as it seemed like a dream, but upon pinching herself, she decided everything had happened as she remembered. Her mother was up and sitting by the window when Amber entered the large family room. Breakfast had also been provided by a servant from the main house. Amber talked with her mother and after finishing her morning bath, Amber put on her best dress which had seen better days, but this Amber decided could not be helped. She would have loved something pretty and new to wear in case Slate was at home but had reflected that he saw her only as a servant and she could not hope to compete with someone as pretty as Rená. She had heard the talk that Rená would be Mrs. Slate King before the year was over.

As Amber had been at the King home and worked previously for parties, she went through the servant entrance and ended up in the kitchen. The staff was having brunch and greeted her warmly. The servants were all aware that Amber and her mother were living at the cottage. Amber immediately went out to set the garden right. She did not consider this work, as she loved being out in the sunshine. She pulled the few weeds from the garden and then cut a fresh bouquet of flowers for the hall table. After arranging the flowers in a vase. she took the flowers into the hall bumping into Slate. He had on his riding clothes and was about to visit various tenants and check over the estate. He grabbed Amber to steady her and the flowers. Amber recovered and pulled herself back from Slate and apologized. Slate only laughed and inquired if she had slept well the night before. She thanked Slate and told him she had slept wonderfully and that her mother seemed to have improved overnight.

Slate could have stayed and talked with Amber all morning. She looked lovely with her hair streaming down her back and seemed almost happy when she was talking about her mother. Slate excused himself and left. He did not want to frighten Amber off by rushing her.

Amber thought that Slate could not wait to get away from her and was only being polite after staying the short time he did and talking with her. Her chores finished, Amber went home to talk with her mother. The next evening a note arrived requesting that Amber and her mother join Slate and Mrs. King for dinner the following night. Her mother said they must attend since the Kings were being so good to them. Amber's immediate problem was what to wear. Her mother seeing Amber's problem, had Amber get the storage box from under her bed. Mrs. Gold opened the box and pulled out a beautiful dress, dark green in color that seemed to shimmer with blue, green highlights. Amber thought the dress was beautiful, but not in fashion. Her mother explained to her that they would work on the dress together and see what they came up with. Amber could not believe her eyes when she tried on the dress the next day. It was made for her, the color did wonders for her eyes and with her hair newly washed and brushed 100 strokes, her hair shimmered like the dress. Amber had no shoes to wear but hoped the length of the dress would hide her feet. When Amber came out for approval from her mother, you could see the love shining in her mother's eyes when she looked at Amber. She told Amber to come over and kneel before her and when she did Mrs. Gold slipped a gold necklace with an emerald heart around her neck. Amber could remember the necklace from her childhood. Her father had presented it to his bride. A single tear escaped her eyes as he hugged her mother for the wonderful gift. With Amber helping her mother they set off for the exciting evening planned. This night they used the front entrance and were shown into the drawing room. Amber's eyes went directly to Slate. He was standing by the fireplace with a sherry in his hand. Since he had not seen her yet she was able to observe him. His shirt was a snowy white with a midnight blue suit. His pants were cut tight and close to his body as was the current fashion. Not many men could wear the style as well as Slate.

Mrs. King welcomed them, and Slate came over. Slate could not keep his eyes off Amber. She was like a vision with a golden halo growing around her hair. Her eyes were like green emeralds in her small face and her whole vision seemed to glow with a fire. Dinner was announced and Slate escorted Mrs. Gold and Amber followed with Mrs. King. Mrs. King observed the fine manners of the girl and how soft-spoken and shy she was at the formal table. She also noticed the looks that Slate directed toward the girl, when he thought he was not being observed. Over coffee, Mrs. Gold mentioned that Amber had taken piano lessons until times had gotten hard and the lessons had to be discontinued. Slate ask Amber if she would do the honor of playing a few tunes for them. Amber was very embarrassed and said she was very rusty as she had not played in a very long time. Mrs. King joined in with Slate so Amber went to the piano. After the first song Amber forgot about her audience and lost herself in the music. Slate could not believe she was such an accomplished player. All the so-called ladies he knew claimed to play the piano but could barely hold a note. Amber on the other hand, played with her whole heart. After much praise Amber and her mother were accompanied home by Slate. Slate asked Amber if she could ride, she responded that it had been a while but yes, she could ride. He asked her to ride with him the next morning.

Amber said yes before she thought, as she did not have a riding habit or boots to wear. The next morning a servant delivered a box for Miss Gold. The box contained a riding habit of forest green with a matching hat with a small feather on the side and a pair of black doeskin boots. She hurried and tried on the outfit. She could not believe that everything fit to perfection. Slate picked her up an hour later. She thanked him for the outfit. Slate told her that his mother had arranged for the gift. She made a mental note to thank Mrs. King.

The horses were ready and waiting when they reached the stable. Amber had not ridden for 3 or 4 years but found she had not forgotten. She felt so good to be riding again with the wind blowing her hair and the sun on her face. It was such a beautiful and perfect day. Amber noticed that the horse that Slate was riding was so big and powerful, just like his Master. A large midnight black horse with a small white streak on his forehead. They had ridden for perhaps 30 minutes when another horse appeared over a rise. Rená instantly recognized Slate but wondered who the girl was with Slate. When she came abreast of Slate, she did a double take as she recognized the servant girl that had previously worked for her. She had wondered what had happened to the girl but had not lost any sleep over her, as she had replaced her with another unfortunate girl. Rená acidly inquired to Slate about riding with a servant. She would not even acknowledge that Amber was present in the conversation. Slate only smiled and introduced Amber and told Rená that Amber and her mother were living at King's mansion at his mother's request. Rená was on the verge of losing control as she noticed the way Slate kept looking at the nothing of a girl. Rená made an excuse to exit before she said something that she would later regret. Rená went home and changed clothes and made a hasty trip over to see Mrs. King. Mrs. King told Rená that she had taken the girl under her wing and how accomplished Amber was at the piano and her other talents, such as cooking and sewing. Rená knew upon leaving that she had to get rid of Amber by any means possible.

One-week later Rená put her plans into action. A party invitation was received by Mrs. King and Mrs. Gold. Everyone was invited to a party and make plans to spend the night. Amber and her mother had decided to decline the invitation, but Mrs. King would not hear of this as Amber had become like the daughter she never had. The dressmakers arrived to outfit everyone, including Amber and her mother.

It had been years since Amber had been able to have a new dress. She and her mother had been letting out or remaking dresses for her to wear. Now she and her mother would be able to choose a dress of their choice. The dressmakers arrived promptly at 11:00 a.m. with loads of pattern books and boxes of beautiful rich material. Amber had never seen so much beautiful fabrics to choose from to make her beautiful dress. The dressmaker and her assistant took both of their measurements and then started the process of choosing the pattern and material for the gowns. Amber's mother chose a rich shimmering gray color material for her gown. Amber could not make a choice for her gown. Slate had ventured down to see how things were progressing and found Amber surrounded by materials and pattern books. Slate saw instantly the material needed for Amber's gown. The color was a blue seafoam color that would be beautiful with her long golden hair and green eyes. The dressmaker agreed with Slate on the choice of material. The pattern was then chosen. Since Amber was so small and petite, the pattern chosen was an empire Greek style, old fashion, yet very up to date.

The dress had long puffed sleeves narrowing at the elbow and ending at the wrist in a v. the neckline was very modest and becoming to a young maiden. The dress caught under her small breast and had yards and yards of material swirling down. The hemline was also in v's all the way around with seed pearls on the v-indentions. The sleeves would also have the seed pearls on the v-indentions. Amber had never seen a dress so beautiful and was so excited that she ran up to Slate and hugged him. Her face then turned bright red when she realized what she had done. She ran from the room to tell Mrs. King how much she appreciated the beautiful dress.

Slate could still feel those little arms around his neck and her small body pressed to his body. He was amazed that she had made such an impression on him. After all, he was a man of the world and had been with countless females, so how did one little girl make him feel so good. Slate then set about ordering shoes, gloves and under garments for each outfit he was about to order. He ordered 4-day dresses for Mrs. Gold and her daughter, four evening dresses for the parties. Small hats for the day dresses and ribbons for Amber's hair. Very pleased with himself, Slate offered a substantial bonus if the dresses were all delivered within ten days, including his mother's order. The dressmaker promised delivery as he requested. She reasoned that they would stop working on all other orders to make sure they were delivered on time. The extra money would come in very handy and would take care of the rent for the month.

Amber ran to the kitchen to tell everyone about her new party dress. Mrs. King was in the pallor and listened to Amber describe in detail the beautiful dress color and style that she would be wearing to the party. Amber told Mrs. King the problem she had been having on deciding the color and Pattern style to order and Slate had come in and made the choices for her. Mrs. King was beginning to notice how much time and trouble Slate was taking where Amber was concerned. She had also noticed that he had been letting his people handle the out of town trips while he stayed home. It seemed that Amber had no linking that Slate was badly attracted to her. Mrs. King suspected that he was possibly falling in love with the girl. After collecting and arranging the flowers, Amber left for the cottage with a small bouquet for her mother. They stayed up late into the night discussing the new dresses and the upcoming party.

Amber could not get over the change in her mother since they had moved to the cottage. It seemed with the right kind of food served each day and the fresh air and sunshine, her mother was coming alive again. She still had to rest a large part of each day but, to Amber she seemed like a different person. Amber had also benefited from the new lifestyle. Her petite figure was beginning to fill out in all the right places.

The next morning Amber was up early, and after having breakfast with her mother she headed for the big house to pick and arrange any flowers needed for the mansion and any vegetables that needed to be picked from the garden for the kitchen. When her chores were finished, she went to see if any additional jobs she could do for the kitchen staff. While in the kitchen the housekeeper asked if she would take a tray with coffee, cream and sugar to Mr. King's office. When Amber knocked on the door Slate bid her to enter. Amber sit the coffee service on the table next to the desk. Slate ask that she pour the coffee as he was in a conversation with another gentlemen. Upon finishing their talk, Slate introduced Amber to his best friend, Giles Meadows. Giles had been abroad for two years and had only returned with the good news that he had married and would be a Father within three months. Amber said hello to Giles and excused herself. Giles noticed the way his friend's eyes followed Amber's movements. He thought that maybe Slate had met his match, at least he hoped so as he wanted his friend to be as happy as he was since he met and married Elizabeth.

Slate had been very happy to see Giles but could not get over the fact that Giles was married and to be a Father soon. Slate was looking forward to meeting Elizabeth since she had made his friend so happy. After Giles left, Slate talked with his mother about a small get together to welcome his friend and bride home. Mrs. King started making the guest list but realized they would have to wait at least two weeks because of the party at Rená's which they had already accepted.

Mrs. King had really thought seriously about declining the invitation as she had heard some very disturbing rumors about Rená from a friend of hers. Mrs. King did not normally listen to rumors unless it concerned her immediate loved ones. It seemed, from the rumors, that Rená was not the innocent girl she claimed to be and if further talk was true, the family was having financial problems and might have to sell their estate. She wondered why Rená would be throwing this large party if all the rumors were true. Mrs. King sent a note to Rená telling her that Giles had recently returned home with his bride and suggested that she might want to issue a special invitation for them to attend the party.

Rená had renewed an old acquaintance over the past month and had secretly been meeting and having an affair with Jim Stanley. Rená had known Jim for a lot of years and he was a very rough and demanding lover, which met her needs completely. Jim had been married for years however this did not stop him from getting together with Rená anytime or anywhere. Jim had the biggest cock Rená had ever seen. It seemed to jump from his pants when hard and pulsed with a life of its own. Rená had sampled many men but none like Jim. She had worried that Slate would notice that she was no longer a virgin when they married but had decided as long as she faked the pain and made sure he saw some blood on the sheets there would be no problem.

René met Jim at their usual place, a long ago forgotten about shack in the woods, south of her house. It was very secluded and off the beaten path. Jim was waiting as eager as René for a little sex. Jim would not even give René time to pull off her panties and bra as he tore them from her body. The brutal act excited René to no ends as she looked down and saw the hard outline of his manhood in his britches trying to spring out and burst free. She reached down and unzipped his pants and his manhood sprung out, large and red with wetness already seeping out the end. René wet her lips as she looked at the instrument that could give her so much satisfaction and pain. Jim was already pushing her head down with instructions. René opened her mouth and took as much of him as she could without gagging. Later he pushed her down on the dirt floor and straddled her and with one lounge he buried himself inside her, she thought he might split her in two. René felt as though she was pinned to the ground at first then she started moving slowly and fire started to burn inside her body. René reached her first climax with a loud guttered cry and ran her fingernails down Jim's back, drawing blood. Jim let out a string of foul words and slapped her across her face. René hit him back and then they were rolling on the floor. His hard member pressed against her stomach. Jim rolled René over and tried entering from the back. René was not ready so Jim spit on his hand and rubbed himself and with one mighty thrust he was in. René screamed with pain on first entry however she was soon joining in the fun. Jim came before René was fully ready, so she instantly demanded that Jim eat her hot pussy. They were finally both completely satisfied and tired. Jim told René she was still the best fuck he ever had. They made plans to meet the following week.

The day of the party was finally here, René was trying on the new dress just delivered. The dress was bright pink with small gold flakes scattered throughout the material. The top was cut very low, showing her breasts and a small part of her nipples. Rená could adjust the dress higher or lower at the neckline, depending on how she wanted to look. The dress had long full sleeves and the bottom of the sleeves and skirt were caught up with small gold ribbons. She planned to have the maid run gold ribbons throughout her long dark hair. Her only jewelry would be the large gold diamond earrings that had belonged to her mother. Her shoes were also gold. Rená glanced at herself in the mirror and thought "Yes" this should get Slate's attention. Rená was prepared to let Slate seduce her before the night had ended and then Slate would be honor bounded to marry her. She had the perfect plan worked out, Slate was to be put in the room adjoining hers and then she would let nature take its course.

Slate had been making his own plans. He now admitted to himself that he was in love with Amber. It seemed that she could walk into a room and it would light up. Her laughter was like music to his ear. He had a present he was dying to present to her before going to the party at Rená's. He could already imagine the way her green eyes would light up upon receiving the gift.

The day of the party finally came, Mrs. King had the maids dress her early and sent them down to help Amber and her mother get dressed. Amber had taken a long leisure bath in oil scented water. When she emerged from her bath her skin was glowing. Amber brushed her long blonde hair until it was dry. When the maids arrived, one started helping Amber and the other her mother. The maid swirled the top and sides of Amber's hair into a crown on top of her head. Tiny strings of hair were allowed to escape and fall down naturally. The back of her hair was left long and shining tumbling nearly to her waist.

Tiny sea foam blue flowers with seed pearls in the middle were woven throughout the top of her hair. Next the silk lingerie was put on and then the beautiful dress. She could not believe she was looking at herself in the mirror. The dress fit to perfection. The color made her eyes glow in the soft light. Slate chose this moment to arrive to take them to the party. When Slate saw Amber, he was sure his heart was in his eyes. He had never saw anything more lovely. Amber was also checking out Slate, his midnight blue coat with a snowy white shirt and midnight blue pants was something to behold. The pants fit his superb frame perfectly, with muscles straining to be unlashed. Amber's breath caught in her throat and wished silently that she had been born wealthy and could compete for his love.

Mrs. Gold came from her bedroom in the lovely gown that added a soft glow to her cheeks. Slate could understand where Amber got her good looks. Mrs. Gold also looked very lovely and was feeling better each day. Slate had the family doctor seeing Mrs. Gold on a regular basis and he had started her on a new medicine that was working wonders.

Slate told Amber she was beautiful, but the gown needed something. Amber was distressed that Slate did not like the gown. Slate then laughed and pulled out the velvet box from his pocket and presented it to Amber. Amber just stood there with the closed box in her hand. Slate laughed and told her to open the box. When Amber glimpsed the emerald necklace, she felt like crying. The green stone seemed to pulse with a life of its own and the diamonds around the stone only intensified the green color. Slate took the necklace and put it around Amber's neck. It looked beautiful as Slate knew it would. Amber ran to the mirror and with a shaking hand touched the beautiful necklace. The necklace was made for her, no one else would ever be able to wear that color without Slate thinking of Amber.

Amber thanked Slate and told him she would return the jewelry after the party. Slate told her that the necklace was hers to keep. Amber was speechless. Mrs. Gold suggested they get started. After picking up Mrs. King they were on their way. Mrs. King commented on the beautiful necklace and Amber told her it was a gift from Slate. Mrs. King now knew something was definitely up as jewelry was a very personal gift. She only smiled and looked at her son with approval. Amber was so afraid that she would do something at the party to disgrace Mrs. King and Slate.

René had been on the lookout for Slate and as soon as she heard them announced she hurried across the room. Slate looked wonderful as usual. René stopped when she saw the snip of a girl hanging onto Slate's arm for dear life. Could this be the rag a muffin who worked for her and could never get anything right and where did the beautiful clothes and fabulous jewelry come from that she was wearing.

René had only included Mrs. Gold and her daughter in the invitation to be polite. She never dreamed that Mother and daughter would have the nerve to show up. She pasted a smile on her face and went forward to greet the party. She reached down and hugged Mrs. King and then gave Slate a big kiss as she pressed her body to his. Slate pulled away as soon as he could extract himself. René then greeted Mrs. Gold and Amber. She complimented Amber on her dress and ask where she had gotten the beautiful necklace. Amber thanked her and replied that the necklace was a gift from Slate. René quickly turned away to greet other guest before she lost it because Slate had never given her jewelry. Slate ask Amber for the first dance. Amber declined saying she was not a good dancer, and it had been a long time since she had even tried. Slate would not take no for an answer and pulled her out onto the dance floor. It seemed to Amber that this was where she was meant to be. She fitted perfectly into Slate's arms. Mrs. King and Mrs. Gold smiled, and both thought they made a beautiful couple as they twirled around the dance floor.

Amber could hardly breath being so close to Slate. Just looking up at him gave her a funny feeling in her stomach. He was so starling attractive and she knew she was the envy of every girl at the party. Slate on the other hand was thinking about how good she felt in his arms. He even missed a step while they were dancing, and this was a first for him. He had always been in complete control, but this little girl without even trying was turning his life upside down. After the first dance, Amber did not have time to get her breath as she was asked to dance continually. Finally, she escaped to the garden to get some fresh air and to catch her breath. Slate, upon missing Amber, found her in the garden. Amber told Slate how much she appreciated all he had done for her and her mother. Somehow, she was in Slate's arms and he was kissing her like he would never let her go. Amber had never really been kissed and was trying to force herself to push Slate away, but it felt so good being in his arms and having her body and lips pressed to him. Amber came to her senses when she felt the cold air hit her back where Slate had undone her gown. Amber then pushed Slate away, begging him to stop. It took all of Slate's self-control to button her gown back and release her. As Amber looked up at Slate, he noticed the tears in her eyes. He gently kissed them away and told her they should return to the party before everyone started talking. As they left the garden Rená stepping out from the tree where she had been hiding, her only hope now was to let Slate think Amber was a tramp and out to get him.

Rená went and instructed the maid to change Amber's room and put her in Mr. Kings room, only telling Amber that there had been a mix up on rooms and she had been moved. The ladies retired around 1:00 am. Amber was shown to her new room and told about the mix up. She noticed that there were still clothes in the room but was too tired and happy to wonder why they had not been changed. Rená knew the men would stay up until at least 3:00 am drinking and playing cards. Slate finally bid everyone good night. He was very much drunk.

He entered his room without turning on the light and stripped down. Slate always slept in the raw. As he got in bed, he felt something warm and soft next to him. As Slate's hands roamed over her body in slow motion; Amber came half awake, but thought she was dreaming as her last thoughts had been of Slate. Slate slowly pushed the nightgown up and his hand closed over a perfectly formed breast. Under his expert touch the small nipple became hard. A soft moan was heard from the small body. Slate captured one of the small hard nipples in his mouth, as his hand moved down to the very core of her womanhood. She was already damp. and her body started moving with a will of its own against his hand. Slate could wait no longer as he straddled her small body and entered. The resistance he met upon entering and the cry of pain from the girl made him hesitate for a moment, but he was too far gone to quit and cruelly plunged himself all the way into Amber. Amber had come fully awake when he had entered, and she had a moment of pain. She now tried to push him off and get out from under Slate to no avail. After the initial plunge Slate slowed down so she could get use to this new sensation.

All at once something started happening to Amber. She felt so warm and wet and it was not hurting anymore. She slowly begun to move matching his movements. Then the movements became faster and faster. All at once Amber was climbing up, up, up and then she reached a point of no return and she went into a stage of peace and relaxation. Slate felt Amber coming and reached his climax a moment after Amber. Slate had not experienced anything like this in his lifetime. He remembered thinking he had to see who this woman was in his bed that had made him feel so alive. Slate dosed for a period of time while Amber lay there afraid to move. Who was in bed with her, and what had she done?

When Slate woke in the early hour of the morning and turned the light on, Amber hurried to pull the sheet up and cover herself. Slate laid there and stared at Amber, a red flush slowly crept up her face and she lowered her eyes.

Upon seeing Amber, Slate was at a loss for words. Amber ask Slate with tears in her eyes why he had come to her room. Slate stopped her and told Amber he might have had too much to drink, however he was sure this was his room. He left the bed and Amber quickly averted her eyes from his naked form. Just to have them return to his beautiful body. Amber had never seen a naked male form before. She had never saw anything as magnificent as Slate. His chest was smooth with only a sprinkling of hair and his chest tapered down to a small waist with strong thighs and rippling muscles everywhere. He had a light tan over all his body. Slate, upon seeing Amber looking at him immediately became aroused. Amber let out a grasp as she saw his manhood in full glory. Slate came back to the bed and gathered Amber in his arms. He was going to make this time good for Amber also. He started running his hands over Amber's body, all the while kissing her lips and perky nipples over and over. When he kissed Amber, she could feel his velvet tongue plunging deep into her mouth making her moan over and over. Amber knew in her heart that this was wrong, but it seemed she had no will of her own. Amber kept climbing higher and higher, reaching for what she did not know. Then the whole world stopped, and she exploded over and over. Slowly Amber and Slate came back to earth. Without meaning to they both drifted off into peaceful sleep, arms and legs wrapped around each other.

Amber came slowly awake she could not seem to turn her head as her hair was caught on something. She carefully turned her head and saw that her hair was caught underneath Slate's arm. In sleep he looked so young and harmless. Amber tried to ease her hair out without disturbing Slate. She wanted to get out of his sight as soon as possible. She felt so ashamed, how could she face him? When she looked again at Slate he was smiling and tightened his hold on her young and beautiful body. Amber tried to pull away which only brought her in closer to Slate. Slate felt his passion beginning to come to the surface again. What was it about this little slip of a girl that could do this to him?

Slate had to find out what was going on, how had they ended up in the same room? He had to remove himself immediately in order to save Amber's reputation. He released Amber and checked the closet to find his clothes hanging inside. Upon questioning Amber, he realized that the maid had probably just made a mistake. He checked outside the door and seeing no one up as yet, he quickly donned his robe and gave Amber a dressing gown and took her back down to the original assigned room where her clothes and belongings were hanging in the closet. He told Amber he would talk with her later. Amber washed off in the bowl of water provided in each room. Going to the bed she instantly fell asleep as her head hit the pillow.

Upon returning to his room, Slate noticed the red stain on the bottom sheet, which confirmed his earlier suspicion that Amber was pure and innocent before his touch and skillful lovemaking had aroused her and made a girl into a warm, giving woman. Slate grinned and went back to bed with a smile on his lips. At 10:00 a.m. Mrs. Gold knocked on her daughter's door as it was unusual for Amber to be sleeping so late. Amber sit up in her bed and greeted her mother with a smile. To Mrs. Golds' eyes it seemed that Amber had grown up since last night. There was a softness to her, and her eyes seemed older and so happy. Mrs. Gold told Amber that she would meet her downstairs for a late breakfast. Amber got up and rushed to the bathroom mirror to see if there was any outward change in her appearance. She knew there had to be! She was no longer the pure and innocent girl that she was last night. She blushed as she thought of all the things, she had done with Slate but could not bring herself to regret a minute of what she and Slate had shared. She only hoped that Slate would not think of her as forward or loose in her way. She had given herself so freely to him.

Amber quickly washed and put on one of the new dresses that Slate had surprised her with before they left the cottage. This one was pink with green flowers, the exact color of her eyes all across the top of the dress. The sleeves were short and puffed with a narrow band of flowers for the trim. She brushed her hair until it shone and added a green ribbon to complete the dress. She floated down the stairs and into the dining room. She smiled and bid Mrs. King and her mother a good morning. Amber was so happy! Slate entered the dining room shortly thereafter and was also smiling and kissed his mother and bid Mrs. Gold a good morning. He then turned to Amber to inquire about her night. Mrs. King and Mrs. Gold exchanged glances something was definitely going on that they were unaware of as yet. The conversation at the table was light and airy with a lot of laughter and smiles all around. After breakfast, Slate ask Amber to go riding with him. Amber excused herself to go get ready. Slate told his mother and Mrs. Gold that he hoped to have some good news for them when they returned home.

Slate ran into Rená coming out of her room in a dressing gown. She quickly grabbed Slate by the arm and dragged him into her room. With a big smile, Rená asked Slate if he had slept good the previous night. When Slate did not answer, Rená told him how she had saw Amber slipping into his room, and what a little tramp Amber was for trying to trap him into marriage. Rená told Slate that she was always having to watch Amber when she worked for her as Amber was always slipping off to the stables to be with the hired hands. As Rená was talking she was backing Slate up to the wall and put her arms around his neck, grinding her body into his and trying to bring his head down so she could kiss him. Slate looked at Rená and wondered what had happened to her in the past 3 to 4 years. At one time he had been sure that him and Rená would eventually marry now his only thought was disgust. He knew now that Rená had set up Amber to make her look bad however the setup had backfired. Slate knew Amber had been completely innocent before he had touched her. Rená was hanging on to Slate for dear life. He angerly pushed her away and started for the door. Rená told Slate that Amber would never have him. She would see to that. Slate dismissed her raving and loudly slammed the door. He met Amber in the hall and told her to pack that there had been a change of plans and they were leaving early. He continued down to the sitting room where he found his mother and Mrs. Gold. He told his mother that they were leaving for home within the hour and he would explain everything later. Mrs. King sent the maid up to pack their clothes. Mrs. King could see that Slate was in a rare state and wisely decided not to ask any questions.

Amber felt silent tears slide down her face as she begun packing. Amber could tell that Slate was furious when he ordered her to pack and she now knew he was ashamed of what had happened between them the previous night and did not want to have anything more to do with her. She finished her packing and left the room. She met Rená on the stairs where Rená informed her that Slate was upset and ashamed of the way she had acted and could not wait to be rid of her. Slate noticed that Amber was very quiet on the way home but did not get overly concerned. Upon returning home the ladies retired to their rooms for a small rest until dinner time.

Upon arriving home there was a message for Slate that he was needed immediately in New Orleans to straighten out some problems concerning their shipping line that could not wait. Slate had to much unfinished business at home to leave now but did not have a choice. He directed his man servant to pack two bags for a stay of at least 7 days plus travel time. His next stop was to see his mother and explain the urgency of his leaving immediately for New Orleans.

Slate then walked down to the cottage and ask Mrs. Gold if he could speak to Amber. Mrs. Gold called Amber down and left the two young people alone. Slate saw that Amber had been crying and guessed wrongly that she was regretting what had happened between them the previous night. Slate told Amber that he was leaving immediately on urgent business and would be gone a week or more. Upon his return he told her that they needed to have a long talk. He would have taken her in his arms, but she seemed as if she was afraid of him. She would not even look at him while he was talking.

After Slate left Amber knew she was right, Slate was leaving to get away from her. He could not stand to look at her after what had happened. Amber should have known that she was reaching for the stars. What she had considered so beautiful was probably something that Slate wanted to forget.

Slate's trip stretched out to more than three weeks. The weeks went slowly for Amber. Her mother could tell that something was dreadfully wrong however when she asked Amber what was going on Amber would only smile sadly and tell her everything was fine. Mrs. King was also, along with the whole household, were very worried about Amber. She had never been big, but it seemed she was melting away to nothing. She was very pale and got sick very easily. Slate had many problems to take care of in New Orleans and did not arrive home until four weeks had passed. His mother was overjoyed to see her only son and the cooks were very busy fixing all of Slate's favorite foods for that night. After bathing from his long trip, Slate met his mother downstairs. He filled her in on what had happened on his trip and assured her that he had taken care of the various problems connected with the trip.

Slate's next question was about Amber. Mrs. King told her son how worried everyone was about Amber, but she refused to see a doctor and said nothing was wrong. Slate instantly excused himself and went in search of Amber. Mrs. Gold welcomed Slate back and told him Amber had gone for a walk and had not returned.

Slate checked the barns and the path in the garden, but no Amber. Then Slate remembered the little lake in the woods where he had first saw Amber. He set off at a fast pace anxious to see for himself that Amber was alright and if not, to drag her to the doctor himself. He was afraid that after finally finding Amber that she was going to be taken away. Slate came into the clearing and saw Amber sitting by the lake and crying. She was so sad that Slate could not stand seeing her like that and knew he would move heaven and earth to see her smile.

Amber saw Slate before he reached her and would have ran, but he grabbed her and held her in his arms until she quieted down and stopped crying. Amber did not know why Slate was with her or why he was holding her so tightly in his arms as if he would never let her go. Slate slowly released Amber but held on to her arm just in case she tried to get away. Slate then told Amber what was in his heart. He told Amber that he loved her and wanted her hand in marriage.

Amber had grown very quiet and still while he was talking. When Slate finished Amber still did not say anything. Slate was beginning to think that he had misjudged Amber's feelings for him. Then Amber looked up at him slowly with tears in her eyes and a smile on her small face. Amber told Slate she had thought he left because of her and what had happened between them. Slate was so relieved, he laughed as he pulled Amber back in his arms. He held and kissed her for a long time. Amber melted in his arms, it seemed with Slate she had no will of her own.

After another long and searching kiss Slate took a good look at Amber. He noticed how pale and thin she had gotten in only four weeks. Slate told Amber he would be having the doctor out to examine her the next day and he was not taking no for an answer. He would hog-tie her if necessary. Amber told Slate she would be fine now that he was home; however, Slate insisted on the doctor coming. After a thorough examination with Slate just outside the door, the doctor smiled at Amber and told her it was nothing serious.

When the doctor left her bedroom, Slate hurried up and demanded to know what was wrong with Amber. The doctor told Slate he could use a sherry and suggested they retire to the study. After receiving his drink, the doctor asked Slate what his connection was to Amber. Slate explained how Amber and her mother had come to live at the cottage. Slate also explained that he had asked Amber to marry him and the wedding would probably be within the coming year. The doctor told Slate that he would suggest the wedding be moved up and the marriage take place very soon. Slate thought that Amber was going to die soon and about lost it. Slate begged the doctor to tell him what was wrong with Amber. The doctor smiled and told Slate that Amber was with child and Slate was going to be a Father.

Upon hearing this, Slate poured a large drink for himself and sit down. The doctor told Slate that Amber was very run down and needed vegetables and lots of love and sunshine during the coming months. He also told Slate he would leave the name of some vitamins that would also help. Slate immediately set about arranging for a wedding. After the doctor left, Slate sit in the study thoroughly stunned. It had never entered his mind that Amber could have conceived from their one night together, and Slate had to get used to the ideal before approaching Amber.

After an hour had passed, Mrs. King went to find Slate and to learn the condition of Amber. Mrs. King and Mrs. Gold knocked on the door to the study and Slate bid them to enter with a big smile on his face. He told Mrs. Gold and his mother that the wedding date would have to be moved up. His mother had always planned for a big wedding for her only son and was disappointed that Slate said he only wanted a few close friends and that the wedding should take place within 2 months. He admitted to the two women that his passion for Amber had overtaken him and the doctor had confirmed that Amber was going to have his child.

Mrs. Gold was disappointed in slate she thought he should have been able to control his desires until he was safety married, however Slate seemed so happy. The two mothers instantly started planning a wedding within four weeks' time. Slate was not ready to face Amber and tell her what he had started when he had taken her in his arms. Amber was getting very worried as the doctor had not told her the problem with her health and no one else had been in to see her. She just knew that God was punishing her for letting Slate make love to her and the delicious feelings she had whenever Slate touched or just looked at her. Slate knocked and entered the room. Amber saw that Slate seemed happy so it could not be that bad. Slate sit by the bed and told her that she was going to be a mother. Amber asked Slate how this happened which made Slate laugh. Amber could not take this in and only laid there looking at Slate. It had never entered her mind that she might be with child. However, thinking back, she had missed her period. At the time she had put it down to worry and the fact that she had not been feeling well.

Amber now realized how stupid she had been and felt a slow flush going all over her body. Slate told her the wedding would take place within the month and both Mothers were working to make it happen.

He told her how happy he was to know that he was going to be a father and that he was going to take very good care of her. Slate was sorry that he had not used better judgement, but where Amber was concerned, he had only to look at her and feel his manhood stirring. He should have given Amber at least a year to get use to him and marriage before getting her with child. Slate left the room and told Amber to rest until dinner.

The maid woke Amber an hour before dinner and told her a tray would be brought to her room. Amber insisted on getting up and dressing and going to eat with everyone. Amber was ashamed to face her mother and Mrs. King, but both made it easy for her. They were both excited and talking about being grandparents. Slate stayed by her side the whole evening catering to her every whim. After dinner he invited her for a walk in the garden. As soon as they were a safe distance from the house, Slate pulled Amber into his arms for a slow, teasing kiss. Amber felt herself responding immediately.

Slate was like the bee and Amber the honey. A look, touch, or kiss made her feel all warm inside with a yearning for more. Slate was also having difficulties. He knew they needed to get married soon, as his feelings for Amber were hard to control, especially after having tasted the delights of her body and knowing how she opened up and gave herself so completely. He thought about all the wonderful things he could teach her about lovemaking. Slate knew it was time to escort Amber back to the house. Perhaps they could have a game of cards. He knew he would be taking a lot of cold showers in the coming days and nights.

The dressmaker came the next week to outfit everyone for the wedding. Slate helped Amber pick out the wedding dress. The dress would be ivory white with a Greek design. The dress gathered under her breasts and fell into soft pleats in the front, this would hide any change in Amber's condition, if indeed there were any in the months ahead. The bottom of the dress had small ribbons every five inches with pearls sewed around the hem line of the dress. The sleeves were long and fitted with ribbons and seed pearls. The neckline was high with a narrow strip of the small ribbon around the neck. The train of the dress extended at least four feet trailing behind the dress with a long lacy veil trimmed with the same pearls as the dress. The dressmaker vowed this would be her most beautiful creation.

Mrs. King opted to go with a light peach long dress, while the bride's mother picked out a darker peach long dress. After the dressmaker left, Slate insisted Amber needed to rest. It seemed that all she did was rest and she was not even two months yet, however this secretly please Amber that Slate was so concerned with her health. Since Slate's return her health had improved greatly. She now had a glow about her face and her figure was filling out nicely. Things went along nice and slow for the next week, and then on Wednesday Rená dropped by for a visit. She had not received the wedding invitation and as yet was unaware of what was happening. She only knew she had to put on a sad face and apologize to Slate for her actions at the party. She would tell him that she had loved him for so long and could not keep her feelings in check any longer.

Rená was hoping to get back on the good side of Mrs. King and thus Slate. When she entered the house, Slate and Mrs. King were in the sitting area of the pallor. Rená immediately hurried over and kissed King and tried to kiss Slate, however he turned his head and she only got his cheek. Mrs. King asked if she had heard the wonderful news. She continued that Slate and Amber were to be married in three weeks' time. Rená could only stare at Mrs. King and Slate and wondered how this was happening, she had to have Slate and his money. She would not be poor. Rená knew she had to win the stakes were too high. Rená knew she had to get out of there so she could plan her next move. She had a lot of thinking to do. Rená knew that if Amber was out of the picture, she would be able to eventually get Slate to her bed and marriage. The trick was to get rid of Amber. She knew that Amber would not go willingly, so therefore, she had to help her along her way and soon.

Rená came up with a foolproof plan but needed to enlist the help of her part time lover, Jim Stanley. She sent word for Jim to meet her the next day at their usual place. Jim was ready and waiting when Rená arrived. His wife had recently had another kid and Jim had no desire to straddle her. After so many children she had no figure left and no passion for lovemaking. Rená suited Jim's purpose completely. She was beautiful, sexy, and liked it as much and as rough as he did. He grabbed her the moment she walked into the shack, they fell together on the floor and Rená tried to get her clothes off in one piece before Jim ripped them from her body. After satisfying their considerable lust for each other, Rená put her plan into action.

Rená told Jim about Amber. Jim remembered Amber and got hot and hard just thinking about her. The little bitch had always thought she was too good for the likes of him. She had come from the poor part of town just like him but had always put on airs like she was better than he was. It would be his pleasure to bring her down a notch or two and maybe let her see what she had been missing by turning him down.

Rená sweetened the plot by offering Jim $200.00 to help her kidnap Amber and after he was through with her he could possibly make some more money by selling her to one of the slave ships going to New Orleans after he had finished breaking her in. Jim saw a way to make double money plus have some fun with Miss High and Mighty. He readily agreed to the plan. Rená told Jim she would work out the details to get Amber away from the house alone and he could take it from there. She also told him that he would need to rent a wagon to transport Amber to the location that he picked out.

The following Wednesday Rená made a call on the Kings. Slate was working so Rená did not get to talk with him. After talking with Mrs. King Rená ventured down to the cottage to see Amber. Amber was in the small garden, so Rená avoided seeing Mrs. Gold. Amber was surprised to see Rená, since she had always thought that Rená could not stand her and was jealous as she had wanted Slate. Rená told her that she had heard about the marriage and wished to congratulate her. Rená told Amber that she was planning a surprise for Slate and ask if Amber could get away the next day and meet her to discuss what she was planning and getting Amber's suggestions as she knew Slate so well. She told Amber how Slate and she had been friends most of their lives and she wanted to do something special for them both. She convinced Amber not to tell anyone as she wanted it to be a complete surprise for Slate. Amber was touched by this gesture and thought she had misjudged Rená and readily agreed.

Amber left out the next morning fairly early before anyone could stop and ask her any questions. She was glad that Rená was going to be her friend, as her family and King's had been neighbors for a long period of time. Amber was looking forward to seeing Rená and finding out what kind of surprise she had planned for Slate. Amber was less than a mile from Rená estate when she saw Rená riding toward her. Rená said she had decided to get out early and meet Amber. She followed Rená's lead and they headed into the woods away from the house. Amber was beginning to think that Rená was acting very strange. After around five more minutes Rená dismounted so Amber followed her lead. As Amber got off her horse, she saw Jim Stanley coming toward them. Rená grabbed the horse reins from Amber just in case she tried to run away.

Amber now realized that she had done a very foolish thing by not telling anyone where she was going. She turned to run but ran into the solid wall of Jim Stanley. His arms tightened around her like iron. Amber looked to Rená for help and saw Rená standing at a distance laughing at her.

Rená said, "You stupid girl, you actually thought I was going to let you marry Slate." She slowly advanced toward Amber as Jim held her fast in his arms. Upon reaching Amber, her hand shot out and connected with Amber's cheek. Rená called her names she had never heard before and continued to slap her over and over. She told Amber that

Slate belonged to her and she would have him and his money. Jim finally told Rená to stop slapping her as he still had a lot of plans for Amber and wanted her awake and know what was happening to her. Amber had a ringing in her ears and could not focus on Rená. It seemed that Rená was laughing and walking away to get on her horse. Amber tried to find her voice and beg Rená not to leave her with Jim, but it seemed that no words could leave her mouth. Jim pulled Amber roughly to her feet. He then proceeded to tie and gag her. Amber realized what was happening and tried to fight him off but did not seem to have any strength left in her limbs.

Jim grabbed one of Amber's pert breast and squeezed; Amber tried to scream but could only moan with the gag in her mouth. Jim threw Amber roughly in the wagon that he had rented that morning to transport her without being seen. He covered her with hay and a quilt before climbing on the wagon. It seemed to Amber that they traveled a great distance. Her arms and legs went to sleep in the cramped position, and she laid there and thought of Slate and prayed he would find her. She thought of the baby that Slate and she had made and only hoped the baby was still alive. Maybe she would be able to reason with Jim once they reached where he was taking her. She figured Rená must have paid him, but she would tell him about the baby and the large amount of money Slate would pay to get her back. She could feel the beautiful necklace under her dress next to her heart that Slate had presented to her and letting her know how much he loved her. Amber dozed for a period of time and only came awake when she was dragged out of the wagon and carried into a warehouse like area and into an empty room. The only item in the room was a bed dominating one wall.

Jim threw Amber on the bed and after checking her hands to make sure she was securely tied, he left locking the door. Amber laid there in the dark room with tears streaming down her face and tried to tell herself she would soon be found. It seemed to Amber that she slept for long periods of time. She did not know if it was day or night, as the room had no windows and it was completely dark. She tried to loosen the ropes that held her bound with no results. She continued to try, but only made the ropes cut into her skin more and finally blood was running from her cuts as the rope got tighter with her struggles. It seemed like she had been there for days when she finally heard the door being unlocked, and a small amount of light penetrated the room. Then she heard a match being lit and the room had light. She had to close her eyes from the bright light, as she had been in darkness for so long and the light hurt her eyes. Her eyes finally adjusted, and she saw Jim Stanley with a bucket and some food. He came toward her and she tried to draw herself into a small ball, away from him. He grabbed and jerked her up on the floor. She slowly sagged down to the floor as her legs would not let her stand up. Jim laughed and told her she was not so high and mighty now and would do well to remember her place and that she was at his mercy now.

He slowly untied my hands, touching my body and grinning. As soon as he removed the gag from my mouth I started to scream. He hit me across my mouth and told me that if I opened my mouth again. I would get hit harder. Plus, there was no one to hear my screams anyway. He indicated I could use the bucket while he laughed at me. He gave me a hard roll and a glass of water at first, I was going to throw the roll at him, but found it was needed to keep my strength up because of the baby. After eating the roll, I ran for the door but found it was locked. Meanwhile Jim was sitting on the bed watching me like a cat with a mouse game he was playing. I told Jim that Slate would pay him any amount of money he wanted for my safe return. I told him I was with child and begged him to release me. All the while he sat on the bed watching me with an evil smile on his face. I finally fell silence hoping he would leave, and I might be able to think of a way to escape.

Then he was off the bed and coming toward me shouting that Miss High and Mighty was going to have a baby by Slate, yet thought she was too good to be touched by the likes of him. He grabbed my dress in front and ripped it to the waist. I tried to fight him with little results. It seemed that I had no fight left and was very weak. I found myself on the bed, pinned under his large frame all the while he was shouting and ripping my clothes off my body. My fingernails landed a long gash to his face and then he hit me again. I slowly feel myself drifting away. When I finally came to, I knew he had used my body to satisfy his animal lust. I tried to hold on to the image of Slate, but that seemed so long ago. Jim was sitting on a stool that he must have bought in while I was out and looking at me. I could see the budge in his pants growing as he continued to look at me. Then he took his pants off and started playing with himself, all the while watching me with that smile on his face. Jim said he had been waiting for me to wake up as he wanted me awake for the second taking of my body. He came over and rubbed his hands up and down my body. I spat at him but only succeeded in making him laugh, then he started biting my breasts and putting his fingers inside me, I screamed as he inserted 3 to 4 fingers inside me; it hurt so much. He took me then over and over, I screamed until I had no voice left. I thought the pain was finally over; however, he rolled me over and entered from behind, it seemed like he was splitting me in to with each thrust. He finally let out a guttered scream and fell on me. After rolling me back over he spied the necklace around my neck. He grabbed the necklace, breaking the chain and also cutting my neck in the process.

I lost all track of time after that and would open my eyes when he threw cold water on me. It seemed that he was there four or five more times, each time degrading me more and more. The baby that had begun with so much love was lost. I lay there feeling the blood run down my legs. I felt no pain, as I had shut off my mind to everything. However, I did feel hot drops of tears running from my eyes as the baby's blood was mixed with my blood.

The next day he did not take my body. He said I was no longer desirable to him. He liked a woman with fight and spirit, and I was no longer anything. I prayed to die and would have killed myself if I had the means. That night he came with a bucket of cold water and proceeded to wash and clean me up. He dressed me in a vulgar dress he had with him. He cut and combed the tangles out of my long hair. He took me out that night and sold me as a loose woman to one of the many ships anchored at the dock. We were to sail that night. Each ship purchased at least 8 to 10 women to keep the sailors happy on the voyage. I vowed that no one would touch me again, if my fate was to die, so be it!

I no longer held out any hope that Slate would find me. After being used by Jim, I did not think that Slate would want to touch me again, and I did not think I could stand anyone ever touching me again. That chapter was closed. I allowed that night of remembering and thinking about the baby that was not to be and knew now I had to do for myself. We women were housed in the hole of the ship we were in a large room with bunk beds lining the walls. We were not chained but had no way to escape since the ladder was taken up and lowered only when we were needed on deck to service the sailors. I found a small pocketknife under the bed and cut my long blonde hair off as close to the scape as possible. While the other women got ready for their evening, I stayed as dirty and unattractive as possible. I took to talking to myself. I was labeled the crazy one by the other women. The sailors did not want anything to do with a crazy person as It was unlucky at sea, so I was thankfully left alone. I never ventured on deck but stayed below in the dark. Maybe I was slowly going out of my mind. I tried not to think of anything. Memories were too painful. When we finally docked in New Orleans, the captain in a hurry to be rid of me sold me to the first bidder who needed an indentured servant for two years. I was only 18 years old but looked at least thirty. I had no thought of returning to my former life, there was nothing left for me anymore. At times I would think of my mother but knew it was better if she thought me dead, as indeed I was.

My employer was not a hard man and if I did my work, I was left alone. I slept in the back of the storeroom, off the kitchen. I cooked the meals for the tavern and kept the kitchen clean. I was kept in the kitchen and not used as a serving girl, due to my appearance. I continued to keep my hair cut off and did nothing to enhance my appearance. Days turned into weeks and weeks into month. Time did not matter to me anymore, I sometimes wondered if I was dead.

Slate had arrived home early and went in search of Amber. She was not in the house, so he wandered down to the stables, still no Amber. He then went to the little lake in the wood all the while calling her name but, did not find her. He found the stable boy in the barn and asked if he had saddling a horse for Miss Amber, the stable boy told Slate he had not seen Miss Amber but that one horse was missing but no one remembered saddling a horse for Miss Amber. Slate was still not overly concerned; he figured that Amber had gone riding and simply forgot the time. After another hour of waiting and still Amber had not appeared, Slate had his horse saddled and rode out to search the countryside. He would have to caution Amber about going riding without someone accompanying her since she was now with child.

After riding for hours and checking the countryside as he rode, Slate saw a horse down by the water grazing on the lush green grass growing there. Slate quickly noticed that this was King stock and was Amber's favorite. Slate called and shouted Amber's name with no response. Slate tried to backtrack over the rough terrain but was unable to pick out any prints on the sunbaked ground. Slate looked for a small figure on the ground, thinking that a snake might have possibly spooked the horse and thrown Amber. He prayed that Amber and the baby were safe and not hurt. After doubling back over the countryside for twenty or thirty minutes, Slate hurried back to the house to get help to search the surrounding area. They searched that evening and into the night, no Amber. The next morning neighbors came and helped with the search. It was like the earth had opened and swallowed her.

Slate continued to search for Amber. Week after week, month after month. He offered a reward of $10,000.00 for any information relating to her disappearance. Slate felt that he would know if Amber was dead, but he had nowhere to start. Amber had vanished. The search had been given up by everyone in the village. The people of the village talking among themselves figures that she must be dead.

It had been well over a year now since Amber had vanished. Slate was a driven man he refused to believe that Amber was dead. Slate had lost a lot of weight and did not look like the same person. He had turned over all the business dealing to his second in command at the office and concentrated only on finding Amber.

Mrs. Gold and Mrs. King were also besides themselves with worry. Mrs. Gold knew that something very bad had happened to her daughter. They saw very little of Slate during this time as he was up early every morning and came home late at night. He was like a man possessed. Slate could not understand why no trace was found. Every time Slate shut his eyes and tried to sleep; he would imagine that he could see Amber in his nightmares calling out to him for help. He had never been a very religious man however now he got on his knees and prayed to the Lord to protect Amber until he was able to find her. Slate checked in with the sheriff regularly, but they had no news to give him. State knew that there had to be a way to find Amber meanwhile he would keep searching.

During this period of time Rená had not given up on getting Slate. She had to have money soon to pay the dressmaker and the other bills for the estate were accumulating fast. Her father had been sick for a long time and was no help. She had borrowed and sold everything that she could to keep up appearance. Rená considered her father worthless; she wished he would go ahead and die, at least the doctor bills would be less. She had started her new campaign by calling on Mrs. King each week and being as helpful as possible in trying to find Amber. In the beginning she had even offered her servants for searching or cooking up large meals for the people searching. Mrs. King had already seen Rená's true colors and was not taken in by the fake concern exhibited by Rená. She now knew that Rená was after Slate; however, did not realize how far Rená had gone to make this happen.

Slate was sure that Amber had not left on her own free will and he would never stop until he found her. The next night he stopped in at the local tavern. His thoughts were of Amber and the night he had seen her there. The local barmaid spotted Slate and hurried over to take his order. She leaned over so Slate would get a good view of her ample charms. Slate barely glanced at the barmaid as he gave his order. She also let him know that she got off at 1:00 am if he would care to wait around and take her home. She indicated that she could make him very happy. After the girl left to fill his order, he was trying to remember something, he had missed something but what? When the girl returned with his beer, he glanced up and saw the necklace shining from the girls' neck. The green stone that exactly matched Amber's eyes. He grabbed the girl so quickly that she screamed and dropped the tray she was holding. Slate yanked the necklace from the girls' neck, breaking the chain and at the same time demanding to know where she had gotten the necklace. No one in the tavern jumped to the girls' defense as they saw a man possessed with determination.

The barmaid was scared and crying and trying to get away from Slate. Slate's eyes were hard cold steel, he would find out the truth. Not a single person in the room moved a muscle. He dragged and half carried the terrified girl into the back room and closed the door. The barmaid cowered away from Slate and begged him to let her pass. She told him he could have the necklace just let her go. Slate slapped her once to bring her under control. He told her the necklace had been a gift to his future wife. She instantly told him the necklace had been a gift or payment from Jim Stanley. He had given her the necklace as part payment for her services. Slate rushed from the tavern on his way to find Jim Stanley. It was already 11:00 pm too late to go calling but Slate knew he had to find out now where Stanley had gotten Amber's necklace.

The lights were off at the small shack at the edge of town where Stanley lived. After repeated knocks the door was opened by a woman, he assumed was Mrs. Stanley. She was in a faded housecoat with small children peeking out from behind her. Mrs. Stanley said Jim had not been home for two or three weeks. Slate headed for the waterfront where he figured Jim hung out. He spotted Jim at his second stop where a small card game was in progress and it looked like Jim was losing. Slate threw the necklace down in front of Jim and demanded in a deadly steel voice where he had gotten the necklace. Jim tried to run but was grabbed by Slate and shoved across the room. Jim was trying to crawl away from Slate as he knew his life was hanging in the balance. Slate hit Jim with two hard punches and grabbed him up off the ground and ask in a calm voice where the necklace came from. Jim could not think and started to cry and begged Slate not to kill him. Slate again delivered a hard punch to the stomach and ask again where he had gotten the necklace.

The whole story came tumbling out of Jim's mouth. His part in the kidnapping of Amber but Slate's mouth dropped open when he heard about Rená s part in getting rid of Amber. He had not thought Rena was capable of what he heard from Jim. Jim said that Rená had paid him for his part in getting rid of Amber. Jim wisely did not mention the raping and all the other things that he had done to Amber. He also did not mention that the baby had died in the process. He knew he would surely die if Slate found out the full story. He only told Slate that he had kidnapped Amber and kept her in a room until he was able to get her on a ship to New Orleans. That no harm had come to her while in his care and he had left her on the ship.

Slate did not have time to deal with Jim and Rená at the present time. His only concern was to find Amber as quickly as possible. He would deal with both of them at a later date. Slate left and immediately headed for the dock to book passage on the first available ship leaving for New Orleans. After getting his ticket for the next day he went home and informed Mrs. Gold and his mother what he had found out. They were both shocked to find out that Rená was involved. He packed his bags and told them he would be gone as long as it took to find Amber and bring her home. It had now been over two years since Amber had vanished and Slate only hoped that she had survived. He would not think about the baby. He kept telling himself that he would know if she was dead. Slate could not think of that possibility.

After weeks of bad weather and rough waves and various delays, Slate finally set foot in New Orleans. He checked with the local authorities to no avail. No one had any information on Amber. He finally offered a reward for any information leading to her being found. Weeks went by and then one day a local business owner knocked on his door. He was not sure if he had information that would help Slate. He informed Slate that he had purchased a woman from a ship around two years ago. He had got the girl cheap as no one else would bid on her and the captain of the shipped deemed her crazy. He had needed someone to help in the kitchen and do the cooking for the dinner trade. He said she had worked well and never gave him any trouble. When she had worked off her debt, she stayed to make some money to live on. He said after she left, he had not seen or heard from her. Slate checked at the docks to see if they remembered her booking passage, no one could help him. Slate vowed to stay until he found Amber.

Slate did not give up. Each day he walked the streets and ask anyone if they knew anything about Amber. One day Slate showed the picture of Amber to a lady and she said the picture looked a little like her dressmaker; however, her hair was really short and unbecoming. He instantly got the address for the dressmaker's shop that was in the poor section of town. Upon arrival the sign on the door said closed until 10:00 am the next day. Slate could barely contain himself but knew he would have to wait until the next day as he had no home address. He was not aware that Amber lived over the shop and was working on a special-order upstairs. He vowed to return at 10:00 am the next morning.

Meanwhile, Amber was unaware of what was going on. She had tried to forget her former life. She had lost their child and was sure that Slate would no longer want her in his life. She also remembered all the vile things that Jim had done to her and knew she could never go back as she was unfit for someone like Slate. So, this was her frame of mind when she unlocked the door the next morning and saw Slate standing here. She could not believe her eyes and tried to close the door before he came in. Slate looked at Amber and felt so sad for all the things that had happened to her. Her hands were red and rough. Her beautiful hair was chopped off and had no life. Looking into her eyes he could see that she was in some kind of suspended shock. He said her name and she turned away and ask him to leave. He had been searching for so long and now to find her like this made him want to cry. He pushed his way into the shop amiss her protest. He tried to hold her in his arms, but she resisted and tried to fight him. He told her she was coming home with him. She looked at him sadly and shook her head and said this was her home.

He figured to give her some time, so he left however was back the next morning. She still would not talk to him. He told her he was not going away and would take her back to their home. He told her how much her mother and Mrs. Gold were missing her. Having no way forward, Amber agreed to go with Slate.

Slate booked passage on the first available ship, but the ship had to make numerous stops on the way back. The trip seemed to go on forever. Amer would not let Slate touch her and demanded her own room. She would not have eaten if Slate had not taken the meals to her room and stayed with her until she consumed part of the meal. He knew that Amber was emotionally broken however he could not understand why she was acting this way toward him. They had been so much in love when she was taken from him.

He had not asked her about their child but figured she had lost the baby with all the hardships that she had suffered. Slate did not know what to do. Maybe when they returned home, and she saw her mother she would be able to heal.

He vowed that Rená and Jim would pay but would take no action until Amber was better. He would devote all his time to making her feel safe and loved. He would make sure the doctor checked her out when they returned home. He would let her mother take care of a proper haircut and a whole new wardrobe. Then he could only wait and hope that she would come back to him.

When Slate and Amber finally arrived at the dock, he rented a buggy to take them home as Amber did not want to see anyone in town. He had been unable to let his mother and Mrs. Gold know that he had found Amber and was bringing her home. When he pulled up at the house his mother came out of the house and upon seeing Amber started to cry. Amber endured the hugs from Mrs. King but only wanted to go to the little cottage where her mother was still living. Slate had to explain that her mother had moved in with them and he would take her to her mother's room, and she could have the adjoining room. Amber slowly followed Slate up the stairs. When she saw her mother she still did not speak or cry only accepting the hugs and kisses of her mother. Her mother ask what had happened to her beautiful hair. Amber finally replied that she did not deserve beautiful and shining hair.

Amber slowly went into the other room and laid on the bed. Her mother ask Slate what had happened to her beautiful daughter. Slate said he had been afraid to question her as he was afraid, he would push her over the edge. He hoped that in time Amber would open up about what had happened to her, until then they would just have to wait.

Amber slept for two days, when her mother heard her stirring around, she knocked on the door with some soup. Amber took the soup and thanked her mother. Her mother sent for the doorman and ask him to take a message to the dressmaker to come and measure Amber for a new outfit as soon as possible. She also requested that the hairdresser make a trip from town to see to Amber's hair. When she checked on

Amber, she saw that some of the soup had been eaten and Amber was laying on the bed starring at the ceiling. Her mother went and sit on the bed and took Amber's hand in hers. She told Amber that she loved her so much, as did Slate and that he had gone nearly crazy when he could not find her and spent all his waking hours and time trying to track her down. Amber finally said that Slate should never have found her. She said she just wanted to die but the good Lord had not answered her prayers. Her mother, crying, held Amber in her arms until the light faded and Amber went to sleep.

The next day the dressmaker came and measured Amber for some new clothes to wear until she had gained her weight back and then they would make new outfits. The hairdresser also came and did what she could with the hair that Amber still had, it would be a while before it grew out enough to really style however, she left with Amber's hair looking better. Amber was still very thin, and her mother was working on getting her to eat more each day. Slate came by each evening however Amber would not see him.

Slate had been working long hours at the office. He was putting off going home because Amber still did not want to see him. He too, had lost a lot of weight and there were dark circles under his eyes. His clothes hung on his large frame and he looked so sad. He did not understand no matter what had happened, he would continue to love Amber. Did she not know this about him?

Finally, Amber's Mother decided she had to make Amber see the heartbreak she was bringing to Slate and the rest of the family. She started by telling Amber how Slate could not understand why she was not confiding in him. She spoke about the baby for the first time and Amber said God punished her by taking the baby. Mrs. Gold ask her why she would say such a thing and that it was not her fault that she had been taken from them. Amber said she was not worthy of Slate's love and knew he would hate her if he knew what had happened to her. Mrs. Gold told Amber she needed to talk to Slate.

Amber said she would not be able to bear the disgust that she would see in Slate's eyes.

Amber stayed awake late that night thinking about all the things that her mother had said to her. When Slate stopped by the next morning Amber could not believe how thin and haggard, he looked. Her heart went out to him and she knew that she still loved him with all her heart and would have to take a chance that he would not hate her after she had told him all the sordid details of what had happened to her.

Amber ask if Slate would stop by that evening when he came home. He readily agreed. That evening Amber took particular pains to make sure her dress and hair looked as good as possible. When Slate arrived, she asks him to sit down and listen to what she had to tell him.

Amber started the story when Rená dropped by to see her and told her she was planning a big surprise for Slate and would like for Amber to share in the details. She asks if Amber would ride over to her home early the next morning and not to tell anyone so it would truly be a surprise for Slate. Amber said she agreed and early the next morning started over to Rená's however Rená met her on the trail. About the quarrel that had erupted when Rená told Amber she would never get Slate that he belonged to her. Then Jim Stanley showed up in a wagon and while Rená held the horse reins so she could not leave Jim overpowered her. She told him how Rená had come after her and kept hitting her over and over while screaming at the top of her lungs. Jim finally told Rená to stop that he did not need her damaged. Jim then proceeded to gag and tie her up, she begged Rená to help her that she was with child. Rena" only laughed and got on her horse and rode away. Jim threw her in the back of the wagon and covered her with straw and a quilt. She was then taken to a small storage building and locked in for days. Amber did not know how long she had been there as it was dark with no windows.

She could not look at Slate as she continued. Finally, Jim showed up with a bottle of water and a hard roll for her to eat. He also carried in a bucket for her to use the restroom. He had a small stool that he put down and then locked the door. He lit a small candle that he had in his pocket.

She had to use the bathroom and ask him to leave or at least turn his back. He untied her hands and feet and waited by the door watching her. She tried to use her dress to cover herself as she used the bucket to relief herself. He sniggered and laughed at her, calling her Miss High and Mighty. He came toward her as she finished and tried to kiss her. She scratched his face, drawing blood. He slapped her across the face and pushed her toward the bed. She tried to fight to no avail, then he was on her tearing her clothes off. He treated her like an animal, biting her breast and squeezing them till they hurt. Then he entered her, and it seemed like he was splitting her in to. He pounded her over and over. After tying her up, he left her.

She was cramping and wondered if he had hurt the baby. He returned two days later and told her he was going to use her over and over, all the time playing with himself. As he started toward her, she begged him to stop because of the baby. He only laughed and continued to rape her over and over. When he left this time, she could feel the blood running down her leg. She knew she had lost the baby. She felt dead inside. She did not know how long she had been there; the days all ran together. She did not react when Jim would come by and take her body. Eventually he tired of her. The next time he came with a bucket of water and a cheap dress for her to put on. He told her to wash and clean herself up. When she refused, he indicated that he could always kill Slate. She slowly washed and put on the cheap dress. While she was getting dressed Jim spied the necklace around her neck and ripped it off. She was then tied and gagged and put in the wagon with the straw and quilt over her. When the quilt was removed, she saw she was at the dock with other women. The captain purchased all the women for his men. They were kept in the hole of the ship and brought out at night as a reward for the sailors.

Amber told Slate she was determined that no one else would touch her. She would rather kill herself, so she hacked off all her hair and would not take a bath and talked to herself. All the women thought she was crazy, and the sailors also referred to her as the crazy one and since they thought she was bad luck would not have anything to do with her. This continued throughout the trip, when they finally docked, all the women were sold. No one bid on her however a kind older man purchased her to work in his tavern. She worked in the kitchen and cooked the meals. After she had worked out what he paid for her she stayed on to make some money so she could live. With this money she started her own little dress shop

When she finished, she looked at Slate and saw tears running down his face. Amber said I know you can never forgive me. He said what do you mean none of this was your fault. He then put his arms around her and they both cried for the baby and for the missed years. He never left Amber that night, they slept in each other's arms. The next morning Amber woke up and looked with love at Slate. She was still in his arms and had been all night. Then he woke up and smiled at her. He pulled her closer in his arms and kissed her. It was wonderful and she thanked the Lord that Slate did not blame her for anything that had happened.

He told her he would be home early. Later that day Amber went to her favorite place in the woods. She laid down next to the lake with the waterfall and let the sun heal her body and mind. Her thoughts were of Slate as she dozed off to sleep.

When Slate arrived home and found her gone, he figured that she was probably at their place in the woods.

When he saw her laying on the ground with her eyes closed, it took him back to the first meeting except she was so much more beautiful now, a woman instead of a child. He leaned down and took her into his arms. By the lake they consummated their love for each other, over and over again. He gently removed her clothes and planted kisses over her body. When he reached her core, she screamed and moaned as he did wonderful things to her body. Her orgasms came fast in wave after wave. She in turn kissed his body and took his large membrane in her mouth and felt him coming, his cum ran out of her mouth as there was so much, she could not swallow it all. They rested their bodies spent for a while. Then they again started touching each other showing their love for each other with their hands and lips giving satisfaction. They slept for a while both wrapped in each other's arms. When they finally made it back to the house Mrs. Gold and Mrs. King could plainly see that things had changed. Amber and Slate could not keep their hands off each other. Amber felt like she had been given another chance with the man she loved with all her being.

Amber vowed to more forward and put the past behind her. Slate, on the other hand, was moving forward however was going to get revenge for Amber at a later date. He had learned that Rená had booked passage on a ship with a friend going abroad for an extended period of time. When she returned, he would do whatever he deemed necessary.

Rená had to leave quickly after Jim told her that Slate was on to them and knew they had taken Amber. She sold all the silver in the house to get the money for her and Jim to pay for the passage. Her father was very ill however, Rená was only thinking of herself and knew her father could not help her. She figured she would have to meet someone on her travels that could help her with the money problems she had incurred. She took Jim with her and told everyone he was her cousin.

At present, Slate's goal was to get Amber well again. By the time their wedding day finally arrived Amber had found out she was with child. It must have happened the evening he met her at the little lake where they confirmed their love for each other over and over. By this time Amber was looking much better and the dress that had been made for the wedding fit perfectly the day of the wedding was sunny and warm and held such promise for the bride and groom. She looked perfect in her long wedding dress. Slate as always looked so handsome.

Amber walked down the aisle with her mother. She thought of her father and how happy he would have been for his only daughter. She was sure he was looking down from above with his blessings. Amber raised her eyes and saw Slate waiting for her. Pure love was in her eyes as she looked at him. Slate was also smiling and thinking about what a beautiful bride Amber made. He thanked the Lord that he had been able to find Amber and that she was safe. After saying their vows Slate gently removed her vail and kissed her upturned mouth and thought he must be the happiest man in the world.

After the big celebration was over, Slate and Amber left on a three-month honeymoon voyage. Amber had never been abroad, and he wanted to show her everything. Slate figures they should not be traveling more than three months as Amber would need to be home close to the doctor and resting.

Their trip was wonderful. They rediscovered each other and shared stories about their childhoods. Amber had never been so happy. They made love over and over never seeming to get enough of each other. Just a touch or kiss could send them back to their suite and rushing into each other's arms for a renewal of their love. Slate taught Amber so much about lovemaking and the different ways she could satisfy him. She was a willing alp student and loved seeing Slate at the mercy of her hands and mouth.

One evening, Amber and Slate had retired to their bedroom. Amber was brushing her long hair and reflecting on the many ways Slate had introduced her to when they made love. She could not get over all the ways he could satisfy her over and over.

Slate interrupted her thoughts and ask Amber to come to him. Amber instantly complied. He then bid her to remove her nightgown and lay across his lap. She did not understand but pulled off her gown and laid across his lap with her dainty backside in the air. Slate first rubbed her backside and then spanked each side three or four times. She was surprised but did not say anything. It did not really hurt that much but did burn and then he started rubbing her and kissing her where he had spanked her. Gradually Amber started feeling warm and she could feel herself getting wet and wild inside her body. When Slate turned her over and started kissing her, she found that she was ready for him and could hardly wait for him to enter her. She instantly climaxed over and over. He then lifted her on top of him and they again satisfied their needs until they fell onto the tangled sheets and went to sleep in each other's arms.

Amber woke the next morning with a big smile on her face. She had learned something new last night that they would have to try again. She wondered what she could do to be punished again!

Even though they enjoyed the time away, Amber was ready to get home and start her new life with Slate. She could feel the baby now and was beginning to show. Upon arriving home, they settled into a routine. Slate did not go out of town and was home each evening. They occasionally went horseback riding but knew that soon they would have to wait until after the baby was born. They wanted no accidents; this baby was so precious to both of them. They went for long walks hand and hand. Everything was perfect for Amber; however, Slate had not forgotten about what had happened and was bidding his time until Rená returned home.

Rená's Father had passed away; however, Rená did not return for the funeral. Slate had learned that the estate was in heavy debt and thought about the possibility of buying the property for the taxes due but had not made a final decision.

About this time, he heard that Rená had returned with a husband. He was from England and was said to be very well off with a title. A large party was given to introduce everyone to her new husband, Slate and family did not received an invitation nor would they have attended if they had received one

It was finally time for the baby to come and Amber went into labor, the doctor was there and had his hands full taking care of Slate. He finally asked Mrs. King to take Slate downstairs. Slate was beside himself and knew Amber would never want any more kids with all the suffering she was going through. He could hear her from downstairs as he paced the floor. It was over eight hours before he heard a cry coming from upstairs. He rushed up the stairs as the doctor opened the door and introduced him to his son. Slate took the small life in his arms and ask the doctor if Amber was OK. The doctor advised him she was fine but needed to rest at present. Both Grandmothers' were begging to hold their Grandson. Slate saw the baby open its' eyes, he noted the green color like Amber and the coal black hair like his. The Grandmothers' got their wish and took the baby from Slate to hold and marble at the new addition to their family.

Slate slipped back into their bedroom and sit by the bed. He wanted to be there when Amber opened her eyes. Around three hours later he noted that Amber was stirring and then she opened her eyes. Her first words were about the baby and Slate assured her the baby was fine. He told her that the grandmothers were both fighting over who could hold the baby. Later a knock on the door signaled that the Little guy was hungry.

Slate watched as Amber tenderly put the baby to her breast and guided the small mouth to her nipple. Slate had never seen anything that could match this picture. Slate later slipped out of the room and thought about all the plans he had for Rená and Jim.

Slate had waited for a long period of time and plotted what he would do when Rená and Jim returned. Now that the baby was here and Amber was safe, he would put his plans into action.

Ever since Rená's return Slate had his people reporting on when she went riding. He knew the pattern that she followed each day. Slate went riding the next morning around the time that Rená always rode. He had not met Rená's husband but had heard he was a Count with loads of money and an eye for the ladies. It was also reported that he ran in dangerous circles and could be vicious when crossed. After riding for around thirty minutes he spotted Rená and two other riders in the distance.

Slate rode to meet them. He introduced himself to the Count. Rená for once was silent as was Jim. The Count was overjoyed to meet Slate and could not understand why they had not attended the party given by Rená. The Count indicated he was really enjoying his stay in the country. He said they were planning to leave in the near future for an extended period of time. He said Rená wanted to see new places and also to do tons of shopping and dining in the most expensive places. He said Rená loved spending his money.

Slate looked at Jim and inquired what he was doing riding with them and what his position was in the household. Rená answered quickly that Jim was her cousin and helped with any problems connected with the estate. Slate raised an eyebrow and inquired how Jim's wife and kids were doing. The Count was taken aback as he did not know that Jim was married and had kids. Slate also told the Count that Jim had lived in the town all his life and was definitely not Rená's cousin. Rená said this was ridiculous and of course Jim was her cousin. Slate told the Count that Jim had left town and deserted his wife and kids leaving them with no money and at the mercy of the State. The Count was beside himself that Rená would have someone like Jim working for her and he also wondered if he was really Rená's cousin as she had led him to believe.

The Count thanked Slate for giving him this information and told Jim he was no longer welcome at their home. He told Jim to pack his bags and begone from their sight. Rená tried to talk to the Count but he was having none of her pleas that she needed Jim to run the estate. Jim told Rená she could not just kick him out; however, the Count was firm and brooked no argument from Jim or Rená. The Count bid Slate goodbye for the present and told him to come over anytime and bring his family.

After being sure the first part of his plan had worked, Slate bid Rená and the Count goodbye for the time being and told the Count he hoped to see him again.

After they got back to the house, Rená went to her room to change and found Jim waiting. Rená told Jim he would have to lay low until she could get the Count to reconsider his words and let Jim come back. Jim told Rená he would not be cast aside, that he could give the Count information that would also put Rená in the poor house with him. Rená told Jim not to worry that she would take care of everything. She told him to slip out the back and meet her at their place the next evening. Jim was not happy with this situation as he had gotten use to the good life and did not want to give it up. Rená gave him all the money in her purse and told him there would be more where that came from when they got rid of the Count.

Slate rode home in a good frame of mind, knowing everything was going as he planned. He met Amber and the baby in the garden. Amber was slowly getting back her strength and looking like her old self and the baby was such a wonderful addition to their family. Amber rushed into his arms for a long kiss while the baby was fast asleep on a large quilt.

At supper the Count was very quiet, which made Rená very nervous. She had previously been able to manage the Count, but this was a new experience for her. Eventually the Count spoke wanting to know why she had passed Jim off as her cousin. He also voiced the opinion that it had not been a good ideal on her part to have been traveling with Jim without a proper escort. Rená knew she had better keep quiet and bid her time.

The Count was not fooled by Rená. He was well aware that she had married him for his money and title. He figured it was a good trade off. He would have a beautiful woman on his arm and be the envy of all his friends. He had now started wondering about the relationship between Jim and Rená after various hints from Slate. He had noticed the looks exchanged between Jim and Rená in the past but had not thought anything wrong at that time. Now he was wondering. He would not be made a fool of by anyone, especially Rená and Jim.

For now, the Count decided to keep his ears and eyes open and see what developed.

Rená was trying to figure out what to do. She knew the Count was getting very suspicious and Slate was not helping the issue with his constant talk about her and Jim. Rená thought about having Jim help her kill the Count and then they would have all the money and she could keep the title as well. She also thought about poisoning the Count; but, knew this would take too long.

The same evening the Count suggested they should have Slate and his wife over for dinner. Rená tried to quickly think of a good excuse for not having them over; but could think of no good reason. She finally said that this would not give her time to make out the menu and get things ready for entertaining Slate and his wife. The Count said he wanted them over the next evening and that she had plenty of time to get the necessary things taken care of. Rená reluctantly agreed to issuing an invitation for the following evening. Rená had the cooks prepare a wonderful meal. Amber begged off and Slate attended the invitation alone. He told the Count that Amber was still not fully recovered from having the baby. The Count told Slate that maybe at a later date he could meet Amber as he had heard so many good things about her.

Rená again did not join in the conversation and pleated a headache after dinner and went to her room. Slate and the Count went into the study with their drinks to talk. Slate told the Count he felt he should tell him what the whole village was saying. Slate said the talk was that Rená and Jim were having an affair right under the Count's nose and they felt sorry for him. The Count was beside himself and wanted to explode with anger; however, tried to maintain and control himself while Slate was there. Slate could tell that the Count was extremely upset over what Slate had revealed to him. Slate stayed on for a period of time making small talk and then departed for home knowing he had accomplished his mission this night.

After Slate left, the Count slowly went up the stairs and knocked on Rená's door. When she opened the door, the Count slapped her hard and demanded to know the true relationship between her and Jim. Rená was taken aback, no one had ever laid a hand on her and she vowed to make the Count pay at a later date. For the present, she started crying and told the Count her only relationship with Jim was as a friend. Jim had always acted like a big brother toward her and protected her always. The Count was taken in by the tears and her plea that Jim was only a very good friend to her and the family. He finally apologized to her and said that possibly he had overreacted and ask for her forgiveness.

Rená readily accepted his apology; but, knew she should do more to throw the Count off. Rená ask if she could sleep in his bed that night as she was very upset and needed his arms around her. So, Rená was back in the good grace of the Count but knew she would have to be very careful. As she laid in the Counts bed after he had ravished her, she vowed she would get even with Slate and also make the Count pay for striking her.

The next morning after sharing breakfast with the Count he announced he needed to make a trip to the village to purchase some personal items and ask Rená to accompany him. Rená pleaded off with a major headache and said she was going to rest. Rená waited until the Count had departed for his trip to the village, she then headed for the stables and ask the groom to saddle her horse immediately and rode out to find Jim. She also had loaded her small pistol and took it with her.

She finally spotted his horse at a dive in the poor part of town. She sent a note for him to meet her at their regular place as soon as possible and that she would be waiting. When Jim finally arrived, she demanded to know what had taken him so long, he replied that he was taking care of some business but was now here. Jim then looked at her and pulled her down to the floor. Rená needed some good sex to wipe out the memory of the Count's attempted lovemaking the night before. Jim was as wild and rough as always. Rená could only think about her own satisfaction and they rolled on the floor with Jim on top and then her on top. Both got all they bargained for in the process. After a while Rená knew she would have to be leaving soon to get back home before the Count. She told Jim he would have to leave town for a period of time while she took care of the Count. That he had gotten very suspicious with all the information that Slate was feeding him. She offered to give him all the money she had with her; however, this did not satisfy Jim. He demanded at least $10,000.00 for now. He said he would not leave until he got the money as he had gotten used to the good life and would not go back to being nothing. When he threatened to tell the Count Rená knew she could not let this happen. She was so close to the end game and getting everything, she wanted. She needed the Count's money and title.

Jim thought he had won when Rená reached for her purse. Rena slowly brought out the gun and aimed it at Jim. Jim saw that he was in big trouble and started begging and telling Rená that he would do whatever she wanted, he told her that he would get out of town immediately and wait for word from her to return. Rená did not believe this for a moment and that he would be asking her for money over and over again. When Jim started toward her, she fired the gun over and over until Jim was on the floor dead. Rená checked to make sure he was not breathing and then put him in the corner with a blanket over him. Rená thought how easy it was to kill someone who was threatening everything she had worked for. She glanced at Jim one more time and then left leaving the door open so wild animals could come and go. With this unpleasant chore over with, she hurried home before the Count arrived.

Slate had been trying to find Jim, but he seemed to have disappeared. After two weeks still no sign of Jim. Slate thought that maybe Rená had bought him off for the present and he had left town until things died down.

The next morning Slate went riding and had ridden for perhaps 30 minutes when he saw the old shack that was on the edge of his property.

He noticed the door was open, the shack was in very bad condition however he did not like the ideal of animals being able to come and go. He stopped and dismounted and headed for the door. The smell hit Slate before he reached the door and he figured an animal had wondered in and died. When he walked in the door, he saw the blanket in the corner with something underneath. When he pulled the blanket down, he could still identify Jim and noticed he had been shot numerous times. Slate was glad that animals had not gotten to Jim and that he had found him in time to see that someone had murdered him.

Slate rode into the village and reported the death. After Jim had been removed, Slate rode back to the shack. He was searching for anything that could explain Jim's death. In the corner on the ground of the shack Slate saw something small shining when the sun hit that part of the floor. When he picked up the item it turned out to be a small earring with 3 large diamond stones. It looked fairly expensive by Slate's eyes if the stones were real. He pocketed the earring and left the shack.

On the way home Slate was thinking that Jim must have been meeting someone at the shack and the meeting had turned deadly. When he again looked at the earring, he determined that it must have been a lady and not the kind that Jim regularly went with. She had to be upper class with money. He figured he would start checking on Jim's whereabouts the next morning. He thought about Rená but dismissed the thought that she would kill anyone.

Slate told Amber about the killing of Jim. She told Slate she was glad that he was dead, that maybe now she could move on knowing that he was finally out of her life for good.

Slate rode back into town the next day but could find no one that knew of any woman that Jim had been seeing. Slate was beginning to realize that the only woman that Jim had been with for a long period of time was Rená. Still he could not believe that she was capable of murder.

The next morning Slate rode into town and went to the tavern and got the address of the barmaid that Jim had been sleeping with on and off.

When he knocked on her door, she was not happy as she had been in bed for only an hour. When she opened the door and saw Slate, her eyes lit up and she invited him in. Slate shut the door and inquired when she had last seen Jim. She made a face and said Jim did not have time for her. He had told her he had a real lady with money and in due time they would be married and leave this place far behind. Slate ask if she knew who the lady was, she indicated she did not want to talk about Jim she just wanted to make Slate happy. Slate pulled out some money for her. She finally said that the lady was rich and was married; however, her husband had all the money and Jim bragged that they had to take care of the husband and then they would have the money and each other. Slate gave her $100.00 as he left.

As Slate rode home he was sure now that Rená was behind the shooting. He wondered what could have happened to make Rená go down this path?

The next morning Slate rode over to see the Count. He asked the groom at the stable if Miss Rená had been riding much the last two weeks. The groom made sure no one was around and told Slate about the Count going into the village and Rená asking for a horse to be saddled soon after. She was gone for around an hour and when she returned gave special instructions that the count was not to know that she had left the estate.

Slate was greeted warmly by the Count. The Count said he was glad that Slate had come by and that they were planning a trip in two weeks and that Rená was planning on selling the estate. She had told the Count that she had bad memories of this place and never wanted to return. The Count inquired if Slate would be interested in purchasing the estate since he owned most of the property joining the estate. Slate told the Count he might be interested and would let him know in due time.

Slate casually mentioned Jim's name and ask if he had been around. The Count said that Jim was no longer a part of their life and was history. The Count indicated that he and Rená had worked out their problems and there would be no more mention of Jim.

ions. Rená took her hand off the gun and left the room over-
that everything had gone her way.

The next morning the Count left early to take care of the arrangements he would set in motion for Rená, his beautiful wife!

The Count went down to the wharf and met with the captain of the slave ship that he did business with on a regular basis. Rená had no idea that the Count made most of his money from slave trading. The captain was a very cruel man and had to be called down sometimes for marking or killing the slave women that he had control over. This kind of treatment ate into their profit.

The Count told the captain that he was going to bring him a woman of class. That he had free rein to make an example of her. He could keep her for himself or share her with the other sailors; but, under no circumstances was she to be set free. He told the captain that the woman liked it as rough as he cared to go. He was aware that the captain loved to tie his women up, whip them, and take them in every way imagined. When the captain tired of the women he would give them to the sailors to do whatever they wish. If she was still alive when they docked, she would be sold to a slave owner to work in the fields for the rest of her life, as she would have no beauty left by this time.

The captain could hardly wait to get his hands on the woman he was already thinking about all the things he would do to her.

The captain was sailing the next evening and the Count said he would have her there.

The Count arrived back at the estate and was very pleased with himself. He must control his anger for now. He told Rená he had been to the bank and had transferred a large amount of money to her personal account. Rená wanted to leave immediately to get the money; however, the Count told her it would take the rest of the day to get the money together and they would have to wait until the next afternoon. The Count indicated that he would take her, and she could get the money in cash or leave it in her personal account. Rena could hardly wait to get her hands on the money and get the Count out of her life. She would have the money and the title. She went to bed that night dreaming of her new life.

The next evening Rená dressed very carefully and brought a suitcase to put the money in. The Count said the bank would wait until they came to town that evening.

When the Count continued down to the docks Rená asked him where they were going. He replied that he needed to check on a shipment that he had ordered. Rená did not question him. Rená told him to hurry, her only thought was getting her hands on the money.

When the Count returned, he had three men with him. They accompanied him to the carriage and all at once grabbed her and pulled her out of the carriage. She was fighting with them and asking the Count what was going on. He told her she was going to take a little trip. He told her that no one made a fool of him and lived to brag about it. By the time they had landed at their next stop she would be well broken in and would no longer be beautiful if she survived the ordeal. There she would be sold to a slave owner, unless the captain decided to keep her on the ship to keep his sailors happy. Either way, she would wish she was dead.

With the cries from Rená ringing in his ears, the Count climbed back on the carriage and went back to the estate where he had a good meal. After a good night's sleep, the Count planned on leaving the next day. He would tell everyone that his beautiful wife had been lost at sea. He would grieve for the respected amount of time and then would continue his life. The Count smiled; he was very proud of himself.

Meanwhile Slate was very happy with himself. He had got his revenge and did not have blood on his hands. Rená had taken care of Jim and he was sure the Count would follow through with his promise to take care of Rena. He did not want to know the details.

Then Amber walked in with the baby. He knew she could see the love shining in his eyes. She put the baby down and came and sit on his nispered in his ear that they could try for another child in a n's time according to the Doctor. She said she had put in an order or a little girl this time.

Remembering all they had gone through, he looked up and thanked the Lord for bringing Amber back to him.

CPSIA information can be obtained
at www.ICGtesting.com
Printed in the USA
LVHW081523100222
710600LV00011B/402

9 781649 134929